AF244309

SEVEN DEADLY PENS 2

MORE DEADLY SHORT SHORTIES

PETER SMITH   **K. BRADLEY**   **MATT C. SULLY**

LARA BUJOLD CLOUDEN   **STEVE MORETTI**

MH TAMMI   **NICOLA HAMER**

Seven Deadly Pens 2
by the KFC Scrutineers

Copyright © 2024 by K. Bradley, Nicole Hamer, Matt C. Sully, Steve Moretti, Lara Bujould Clouden, Peter Smith and Merja Tammi. (The KFC Scrutineers)

All rights reserved. *(v. 1.0)* No part of this book may be reproduced in any form or by any electronic or mechanical means, including information storage and retrieval systems, without written permission from the authors, except for the use of brief quotations in a book review.

Published by DWA Media - Ottawa, Canada

CONTENT NOTE

This book contains potentially triggering subject matter, including discussions of self-harm.

If you are struggling, tell someone who can help.

Canada:
https://www.canada.ca/en/public-health/services/mental-health-services/mental-health-get-help.html

USA:
https://www.apa.org/topics/crisis-hotlines

UK:
https://www.nhs.uk/nhs-services/mental-health-services/where-to-get-urgent-help-for-mental-health/

Or reach out to your local resources.

CONTENTS

MORE DEADLY STORIES

Be sure to check out the first

7 Deadly Pens

short story collection.

If you dare…

SEVEN DEADLY STORIES

Lake Nicaragua *(Peter Smith)*

When a biologist with an unwavering commitment to ethics is asked to greenwash a massive engineering project in Central America, he is driven to the breaking point, with terrifying consequences for his greedy employer.

FACE *(K. Bradley)*

Rayne, feeling disoriented in the unfamiliar surroundings of her hospital bed, longs for the comforting embrace of FACE. But is it truly the sturdy, beloved tree from which she's always sought shelter, or is there something darker lurking beneath its gnarled roots?

A Good Man *(Matt C. Sully)*

When a DNA analysis company reveals him as genetically predisposed to murder, William Powell is forced to confront his own nature to clear his name. Can he remain the good man he thinks he is, or is he bound by science to become a killer?

Brokenhearted *(Lara Bujold Clouden)*

Sandra's granddaughter arrives with a boyfriend who looks eerily like the lover she lost to tragedy forty years ago. Some memories should remain buried—especially those that refuse to stay dead.

Digital Diva *(Steve Moretti)*

Julie created an AI companion filled with her troubled memories and able to analyze twenty trillion bytes of data per second—a marvel of technology designed to serve others until the bot decides on a new mission: replacing its creator.

A Sailor Went to Sea *(MH Tammi)*

Agatha Christie fan, Martha, sees mysteries everywhere, but never expects to be in the middle of one. A cruise with long time friends reveals that nothing is at it appears. As they sail from port to port, and the mood turns darker, she unwittingly becomes the catalyst that will change all of their lives.

I.C.U. *(Nicola Hamer)*

I.C.U. psychosis: a disorder in which patients in an intensive care unit experience a cluster of serious psychiatric symptoms. It usually resolves when the patient leaves the I.C.U… Usually.

Peter Smith

LAKE NICARAGUA

Primordial fears exist for a reason

LAKE NICARAGUA

PETER SMITH

Victor's kayak skimmed along the glassy surface in a lonely part of the vast lake, the air sultry and unusually still for late afternoon.

A deep, guttural growl drew his gaze to a howler monkey perched in a fig tree on the nearby shore. Despite its name, the monkey's call was less a howl and more a low-pitched Gregorian chant from someone with indigestion.

After listening to the simian serenade for a minute, Victor looked in the opposite direction at a distant island from which rose two colossal volcanos, one ringed with smoke. Beyond the island, sapphire waters stretched to the horizon.

Through the eyes of a tourist the exotic scene would be idyllic. Victor, however, was not a tourist; he was working, and where others saw beauty in the dark blue water, he saw a darkness that chilled his soul.

Dipping the right blade of his paddle into the lake, he pulled back with a smooth, measured sweep. He duplicated the action on the left, the alternating strokes propelling him in a straight line leaving minimal wake.

Thanks to expert precision and efficiency, he could easily double his speed; instead, he held back for today's guest, who sloshed along in a separate kayak behind him.

Victor looked over his shoulder and called, "How you doing?"

Doug Ladron, face red with determination, stabbed the water with his paddle, jerking his boat from side to side. He paused, leaning his paddle's shaft across the kayak, and panted, "How the hell does it look like I'm doing?"

"Better than when we started, but you need to balance your strokes and get into a rhythm."

"Says the wildlife biologist who was practically born in a canoe."

Victor's weathered face and athletic build indeed matched his love for paddling. Meanwhile, Doug, Chief Communications Officer of Burtoni Engineering, who seldom strayed from the boardroom, also had a physique proportionate to his interest in outdoor activity.

"And look at the equipment I'm using," continued Doug. "You're riding in the Cadillac of kayaks with a sturdy paddle, while I'm in a tipsy piece of shit, using this flimsy thing." He shook his paddle. "I might as well be paddling with a pool noodle."

"I imported a high-end kayak for myself when I first arrived here, because this is my daily work vehicle for three months. You're here for a brief visit, so what you've got is all that's available around here for a one-day rental."

Victor slowed and pivoted his kayak to face his exhausted guest. "Tell you what, we'll rest here for a minute."

"Good," gasped Doug as he cupped water with a hand and splashed it on his face and neck. "I can't believe I let you talk me into flying down here to do this." After a few deep breaths, he looked around and frowned. "By the way, why is this place so graveyard quiet? I haven't seen a boat since we left the dock."

"For starters, pleasure boating isn't a common part of the local culture like it is back home. There's also a scarcity of tourists thanks to Nicaragua's perceived violent crime rate and political instability—key word being perceived. The result is a small number of boats on a lake covering 8,000 square kilometers."

"What a waste. I mean…look here." Doug swept a finger back and forth at dense tropical wilderness on shore. "There should be hotels all along this stretch, and a marina in that bay."

"You're pointing at a protected nature reserve, but I'm not surprised to hear that you would clearcut the jungle to make way for a resort."

Doug snorted and leaned back to stare at the sky while massaging his left shoulder. "How much further do we have to go?"

"If we maintain our speed, I'd say less than thirty minutes."

Doug's gaze snapped from fair-weather clouds back to Victor. "Thirty more minutes? We've already been out here that long, and before we started, you told me the entire trip would be about half an hour. How did thirty minutes become an hour?"

"I didn't realize we'd be traveling so slowly."

A swing of Doug's paddle sent a shower of water over Victor. "If you have such a tight schedule, then why are we kayaking? We could have driven to the village."

Victor suppressed a smile while wiping lake water from his face. "Think about the optics. What could look better than the Chief Communications Officer arriving at an indigenous fishing village in a pollution free boat? Besides, I want you to actually experience some of the ecosystem your company pretends to care about."

"Let's get something straight. I agreed to join your little

charade down here as a publicity stunt. That's all. I'm not interested in a biology lecture."

"Little charade?" Victor pursed his lips and looked away for a moment in search of composure, then turned back to Doug. "Do you have any idea how much effort I've put into this research report? We aren't talking about a little drainage ditch behind a factory. You guys are asking me to greenwash a project that'll affect Central America's main freshwater reservoir. And now that I've studied it in person, I'd say its even more fragile than I expected. There's no way you can run a canal through here to connect the Atlantic and Pacific without causing massive ecological change. You're going to need a miracle to convince credible scientists otherwise."

Doug leaned toward Victor and whispered, "I'm going to let you in on a little secret." Then he barked, "Credible scientists don't matter here! We only have to convince the local government, because they make the final decision. They're corrupt and desperate for investment, so they'll happily rubber stamp a bogus environmental study. You only need to make your report look good, and you're the perfect guy to do it, what with your upstanding reputation in academia."

"But there's the catch. If the report I'm writing miraculously leads to an approval, everyone in my field will know that I fabricated the data. As a consequence, my reputation will be toast when I go looking for my next research contract."

"With the amount of money you stand to make if this deal goes through, you'll be able to fund your own research. So stop worrying about integrity."

Money, thought Victor as he looked toward the smouldering volcano in the distance. His wife Jez had grown weary of watching his sporadic research grants dry up, to the point where she refused to start a family until they had more financial stability. His marriage strained, Victor took the Burtoni contract and its prospect of a dazzling payoff.

"It's interesting," said Victor, "that regardless of whether this project gets the green light, you'll still receive your base salary of $400,000. I, meanwhile, work like a dog on a term contract thousands of miles from home, while living on a pittance and a bunch of stock options that are worthless unless Burtoni's share price increases dramatically. I've also learned that Burtoni put all its marbles into this canal project, which means I get squat if the project isn't approved. Correct?"

Doug nodded. "It's a high risk, high reward scenario, and that's why I'm confident you'll write up a convincing, environmental report that'll make Burtoni's shares skyrocket."

"Ethics versus profits."

A chuckle rumbled deep in Doug's chest. "Welcome to the real business world, college boy. Seven years of university and you just figured that out?"

Victor's knuckles turned white as he squeezed his paddle. He glanced at his diving watch. "Let's get going. I left a buffer of time in case we were slow, but it's getting tight and I want to be early for our meeting."

He swiveled 180 degrees, then resumed paddling with Doug struggling along beside him. After a few strokes Victor said, "Even if I write up a pretty report that satisfies the government, there's still the issue of the indigenous population. A glossy document won't fool them. They know a canal would destroy their fishery and force them to relocate. It'll be cultural genocide."

Doug rolled his eyes. "You don't think we've considered that angle? Like natives everywhere, they'll talk a storm about their traditions and culture and all that bullshit, but deep down all they want is money. We've already done the math, and we can justify a one-time payout to every single Indian down here that'll be equivalent to ten years of their paltry fishing income. When they hear that, they'll come around."

"It's possible, but you may be underestimating the fact that they view fishing as more than a job; it's a way of life, and this lake is their lifeblood."

"Oh, spare me."

Victor shrugged. "Just saying." He took a few more strokes, then added, "Actually, the particular indigenous group that I've gotten to know has been incredibly helpful. What they lack in formal education, they make up for with deep knowledge of the region's history."

"That's nice."

"Seriously, this place is incredibly unique. For example, despite this being a freshwater lake, there used to be sharks here."

Doug stopped paddling and glared at Victor. "That's not funny."

"Huh?" Though Victor did indeed remember Doug's phobia, he stared pensively at Doug for a moment, then slapped himself on the forehead. "Oh, that's right. I forgot that you have a thing about sharks."

"Not just a thing; I developed a pathological fear of sharks as a child, and I clearly remember telling you that when we first met."

"Yes. Now I remember. When I was being interviewed, I told you about my work in marine biology, and you brought up the topic of sharks. But tell me, I don't think you ever explained how you developed that fear in the first place."

Doug's shoulders sagged. He set his paddle across his lap and massaged his forehead. "I hate discussing this, but I'll give you the abridged version if you promise not to ask me any more about it."

"I promise."

Doug resumed paddling slowly, a dazed look spreading across his face. "When my family was on vacation in Maine, for some bizarre reason my parents thought it would be a good idea to let their 5-year-old stay up and watch the movie Jaws with them before bed. The next day, we went on a budget fishing excursion on the ocean, and then promptly sank. We bobbed in the waves for over an hour waiting to be rescued, and although my mother claimed it was my imagination, I swear I saw a shark fin in every second goddamned wave that rolled past us while we waited. We survived physically, but I was in and out of psychotherapy for years."

"Hmpf."

Doug snapped out of his trance and scowled at Victor. "What do you mean by hmpf? I was so traumatized it took me about three years to get up the nerve to try swimming in a backyard pool."

"Sorry. I didn't mean to belittle your childhood trauma."

"Good. And don't forget it."

"I promise not to forget it. Now, back to local history. There are different theories on how the lake evolved, but the leading theory is that this used to be part of the Pacific until massive volcanic eruptions sealed it off from the ocean. After that, it gradually lost its salinity. The only remaining connection is the San Juan River that empties into the ocean." Victor pointed his paddle over the tip of his bow. "It's down that way, past our destination."

"Well, I'm glad to hear that we're in fresh water now, because one of the coping mechanisms my therapist and I agreed upon was to simply avoid the ocean, since that's where sharks live. I also learned to accept, after having it drilled into my head by the therapist, that Jaws is a fictional story."

"Actually, Jaws has a true life parallel known as the Jersey shore shark attacks."

"Shut up."

"I'm serious. During a twelve-day period in the summer of 1916, a rogue shark attacked five people in New Jersey, killing four of them. And get this: three of the attacks occurred in a freshwater creek."

With eyes closed and teeth clenched, Doug growled, "I mean it. SHUT—YOUR—MOUTH!"

"Fine, but let's pick up the pace."

They paddled in relative silence for another twenty minutes until they reached an inlet marked with a weathered signpost, its faded message written in Spanish.

"We turn here," said Victor.

As they paddled into the mouth of the river past the sign, Doug asked, "What does that say?"

"It's a sort of unofficial warning that this waterway is claimed by an indigenous tribe. Fortunately, they gave me permission to visit, and we don't have far to go."

"Good."

The river took a sharp bend to the left, then an immediate U-turn to the right, widening into a deep pool hidden from view on the main lake by a high bank forming the switch back.

"And this is where we wait," said Victor as he led Doug to the center of the pool. He checked his watch. "They should be along soon from that direction." He pointed his paddle at the opposite end of the pool where the tributary narrowed and snaked its way upstream, disappearing under tropical foliage drooping from the banks.

"This is the deepest, widest part of the river," said Victor, "so the current is very weak here making it easy to hold your position by sculling your paddle like this."

He demonstrated a simple technique of feathering the surface to counterbalance the gentle flow of water.

Doug followed suit, and the two kayaks held steady.

"How primitive are these people?" asked Doug.

"They won't be wearing loin cloths and paddling a dugout canoe, if that's what you mean. But they are poor. They harvest fish from the lake and the estuary that leads to the ocean. Then they take their catch to the village several miles up this river to be cleaned for sale at the market."

"I don't suppose they speak English."

"No, but I can translate."

A distant hum pulled both men's attention upstream. The buzz of an outboard motor grew louder until a long, thin boat nosed around a bend, slowing as it entered the deep pool. When near the kayaks, the engine stopped altogether, dropping its bow and displacing a wave that gave Doug a moment of panic as he tried to stabilize his tiny vessel.

The motorboat contained two swarthy young men in tattered t-shirts and shorts. A cigarette drooped from the mouth of the one operating the motor in the stern, while the man in the bow sported a faded Yankees ball cap.

Victor nodded toward the men and called out, "Buenos tardes."

The two men nodded back and said, "Tardes." They began shifting pails around on the floor of their shallow boat.

"So, they were expecting us, right?" asked Doug

"Yup."

"Well, aren't we going to shake hands and chat with them about the project?"

"First, I want you to see part of their daily ritual."

Each fisherman struggled to hoist a pail onto the side of their boat, eventually pouring a lumpy red slurry into the water.

"What are they doing?" asked Doug. No sooner had the words left his lips than a stench filled his nostrils. He clamped a hand over his mouth and nose. "And what is that smell?"

"Cleanings from the day's catch: heads, entrails, and so on.

As you can imagine, they wouldn't want to dump it upstream near the village where they bathe and get drinking water, so they bring it here."

A thin, triangular object broke the surface between the kayaks and the boat, zipping through the water for a few seconds before resubmerging into the dark pond.

Doug's gaze was fixed on the residual ripples from the brief apparition. His lip quivered for a moment. "What was that?" he asked in a feeble voice that broke on the last word.

Before Victor could respond, the fin reappeared, followed by another coming from the opposite direction, both slicing through the surface toward the spreading slick.

"Behold," said Victor, his hand sweeping in a flourish toward the aquatic visitors, "Lake Nicaragua's fabled sharks." He watched Doug sit in silence, jaw agape, wide-eyed stare riveted to the red stain in the water where three fins now circled.

Victor let Doug's trance deepen for half a minute before adding matter-of-factly, "Bull sharks have the rare ability to adapt to fresh water. That's why it's the species theorized to have terrorized New Jersey in that story I told you earlier."

"Sharks," hissed Doug. He half turned his head toward Victor, while maintaining an eye on the unfolding aquatic spectacle. "You said there used to be sharks here—past tense. You tricked me."

"Tsk tsk tsk. Imagine me being unethical. How else was I going to get you here?"

"You lying prick."

"Oh, come on." Victor chuckled. "Surely your psychologist told you that the path to freedom from anxiety is directly through that anxiety. You've got to face your fear if you want to get over it. Besides, you're fortunate to see such a rare sight, because Nicaragua is one of the world's only freshwater lakes inhabited by bull sharks. We're very lucky to have this special invitation, because even the other locals don't know about this particular spot."

"Lucky?" Doug's gobsmacked stare darted from the water to Victor.

"Yes, lucky," said Victor. "It wasn't until the indigenous people realized I was genuinely interested in their plight, and not a threat, that they showed me this. My working theory for the origin of the sharks is that females migrate up the San Juan estuary from the ocean to give birth in a sheltered location with few predators, and since this also happens to be where the fishermen dump their waste, it provides a perfect food source until the young sharks are large enough to go to the ocean. That's why you'll see a lot of smaller fins, but also the odd massive adult female as well."

As the fishermen dumped more pails, the water teemed with sharks battling for each morsel, tails thrashing, teeth gnashing at fish heads on the surface. As if on cue, the smaller fins scattered as a huge dorsal fin knifed toward the frenzy.

"And there's a big mama now," said Victor.

"Oh my God," said Doug breathlessly.

"Relax, Doug. As long as you're in a boat you should be safe, so sit back and enjoy the show."

"No. I've got to go ashore—NOW!" Doug smacked his paddle on the surface.

"I wouldn't recommend doing that," said Victor in a sing-song voice. "Any splashing could attract them, and that's the last thing you want to do in the midst of a feeding frenzy. You see, although sharks don't like the taste of all the iron in human blood, if you fall in here, you'll be basted in fish blood, which they love."

Doug pulled his paddle clear of the water, eyes frantically scanning the vicinity of his kayak.

Their final pail emptied, the fishermen took their seats. With a pull of the starter cord, the motor burbled to life and the boat slowly veered away from the churning slick of chum. The man in the bow lifted his cap by its bill and nodded to Victor.

Victor waved and said, "Adios." Then he and Doug watched the craft round the nearest bend upriver.

As the whine of the motor faded, Doug asked, "Aren't we going to follow them to their village?"

"Eventually," said Victor, "but not just yet. It's still not safe to start splashing. We need to wait until they've quieted down a bit more. In the meantime, I want to discuss a different topic." He cleared his throat. "Tell me, how does it feel to be single again?"

"What?" snapped Doug, still staring at the creatures battling for the remaining carrion. "What a time to ask about that. Who the hell cares?"

"I'm just wondering if you're getting much action since your divorce?"

Doug half turned toward his colleague, but stopped short of making eye contact. For the first time since the appearance of the sharks, Victor seemed to have drawn Doug's attention away from the water.

"What do you mean?" asked Doug, his voice lower and measured.

"Well, I'm not sure my marriage is going to last either. I used to think I had a good relationship with Jez, but earlier this year I sensed that she was becoming distant. Do you remember meeting her at the office party?"

Though still not making eye contact, Doug said, "I…I think so."

"You think so? Perhaps you thought I wasn't perceptive, but I watched your eyes tour my wife's tight shirt that night. Then you really chatted her up when you got her alone at the bar. And on our way out at the end of the evening I saw the knowing glances you two exchanged. It was only a few weeks later that you conveniently announced you were sending me down here for three months, so I decided to play along, but, before I left, I hired a private investigator ... to keep an eye on things back home."

Victor sculled with his paddle, slowly drawing the boats together until he was behind Doug, but close enough to reach out and touch him.

"I saw some pictures from your little getaway together in Montreal," said Victor as he scanned the inlet and outlet points of the pond to confirm their solitude. Then he asked through gritted teeth, "How did you enjoy my wife?"

Doug sat frozen, staring straight ahead while weighing the two dangers surrounding him—one behind, the other lurking beneath. As adrenalin kicked in, he plunged his paddle deep into the water in a desperate attempt to escape. But his clumsy effort barely moved the kayak before the thin edge of Victor's paddle caught him in the back of the neck, stunning the hapless executive.

Doug slumped forward, head lolling to one side, revealing a fierce red welt already swelling on his neck. He was motionless now, hanging over the side of the boat, left arm and shoulder dangling in the water, and his paddle floating several feet away.

After a 360-degree check to confirm they were still alone, Victor set his paddle between his legs. Careful not to capsize himself, he managed to help Doug the rest of the way out of the kayak, easing him headfirst into the pink froth.

A small creature darted in for an exploratory bite, followed by another, gradually leading to the resumption of a frenzy.

Victor experienced an involuntary shudder while watching Doug's body twitch as small pieces of flesh were torn from it. His anxiety didn't ease until a larger animal bit into the crook of the neck where it met the shoulder, and then shook violently, tearing off a ragged piece of flesh, thereby eliminating evidence of the bludgeoning.

After carefully cleaning the blade of his own paddle, Victor gripped the rear of Doug's empty boat and flipped it over to complete the accident scene.

While gently backing away, he watched Doug's torso roll over in the boiling water. Then Victor took a deep breath and quietly paddled around the bend to the open water of the lake.

Having calibrated the distance beforehand, he stroked leisurely on his journey toward the nearest home on shore. His plan, when close to the dwelling, would be to sprint the last hundred yards to ensure he was breathless when he began his show of tearful panic, begging the inhabitants to call for rescuers.

But with a twenty-minute paddle ahead of him, there was still time to dream about how to capitalize on his wife's fear of snakes.

- ❧ -

ABOUT PETER SMITH

After dreaming up stories for years, Peter finally decided to put his thoughts on paper. Published short stories thus far include *A Perfect Memory* and *Lake Nicaragua*, both found in the multi-author anthology series *Seven Deadly Pens*.

He is currently working on a medical suspense thriller trilogy, anchored by his debut novel, *The Mantis and the Monarch*, in which the chaotic world of cancer research becomes entangled with bioterrorism.

On cold winter nights, Peter can be found sitting in front of a fire on a small family farm in Ontario, Canada, trying to tame his imagination with a pen.

Email him at fairweatherfarming@gmail.com

K. Bradley

FACE

It watches in petrified silence

FACE

K. BRADLEY

FACE has two eyes. They are asymmetrical. The left bulges forward. Its crusted lid flaps haphazardly against the wind. The right eye, lower than the left, is pushed back like a stepped-on soda can. There is no nose, only chiselled skin in checker box rows that crawl with ladybugs. Their ruby shells glisten against the waning September sun. The mouth has a lopsided gape. It reminds Rayne of the butternut squash at the market.

Today Rayne will try once again to touch FACE. She pushes her foot forward but her toes are trapped under the tight sheet. Her foot slips and FACE is gone. And like every time FACE vanishes, she is returned to the white nothingness and the whooshing breath.

Rayne fades into the blankness for a second, a minute, an hour, and prays for FACE to reappear. Instead, she is interrupted by the man. He has an accent that makes her think he is French. When the man comes she can never see FACE. When the man comes the whooshing breath always gets louder.

When the man comes, sometimes, it hurts.

Today the man is kind and his words are starting to blend and make sense. Rayne is curious about the words but longs to escape and find FACE again, although, in her heart, she knows FACE is only a memory.

THE FIRST TIME RAYNE SAW FACE WAS TEN YEARS AGO. IT WAS THE day the fighting stopped and she couldn't stand how thick the air hung in gaping silence. It was the eighth day in a row that Mommy and Daddy fought. Rayne knew it was day eight because it was her turn to pull the foil-wrapped chocolate from the wooden advent calendar. Days that were odd numbers were her little brother Aiden's days and even-numbered days were Rayne's. Rayne loved this, not only for the delightful treat but also because she had learned about even and odd numbers in school and could show off knowing which days were hers.

That night, the eighth night of her parent's fighting, Grandma pushed her chair back in frustration from the yelling that flooded down the stairwell. She pushed back so hard that her teacup wobbled and defied gravity for a moment before landing perfectly intact. Then she stormed upstairs and gave Mommy and Daddy a 'piece of her mind', which apparently worked as the house was overcome in the eerie quiet.

"Come children." Grandma extended her hands in each direction, one for Aiden and one for Rayne. "Let's go for a walk."

As the three walked through a dusting of snow along the suburban path, Grandma explained that sometimes adults had things to deal with and Mommy and Daddy needed time to work those things out.

It was about fifteen minutes into the walk when FACE appeared. Thirty feet to the left of the path, the gnarled tree behemoth stood higher and wider than any others. Its roots lay like tangled cords above the surface of packed ground. The smallest roots reached upward with long deformed fingernails.

"Grandma, look!" Rayne let go of Grandma's hand and ran toward the tree. "It looks like a person!"

Aiden followed, slapping the tree with his tiny hand and grinning. "It's so big!" he said.

"Well, Rayne, you're right." Grandma moseyed gingerly across the brush and snow. "You sure do have an imagination but I can kind of see a face in the bark too!"

Rayne placed her flattened hand against the cheek of the tree's face, staring into its eyes in wonderment. "It's so big and tall!"

"Must be one of the original trees," Grandma explained, "from back when this neighbourhood was a forest. Most were cut down to build the houses twenty years ago, but this one, my goodness. I've walked by it many times but never noticed the _"

"FACE!" Rayne squealed and wrapped her arms around its trunk, too wide for the stretch of her arms to meet. She felt it then, a vibration emitting from the cool bark, an energy that told her everything would be all right.

"FACE is here to watch over us," Rayne announced.

Grandma frowned. "Perhaps." She took in the tree's features, captivated by Rayne's imagination. "Now, let's keep walking before it gets dark." Grandma started back down the path turning back for the children and freezing in mid-step, her eyes facing the tree.

"What is it, Grandma?" Rayne asked.

"Oh, nothing dear." As Grandma turned and led the children away, FACE lowered its gaze and a droplet of water escaped its left eye.

Later that night Rayne snuggled into Grandma's warm body. Rayne stroked Grandma's soft white hair that fell in soft swirls at the base of her neck. Rayne longed for Grandma to stay longer than this two-week visit.

Aiden was on the other side of Grandma, whose shelf stomach perched a bowl of fluffy popcorn as her arms extended around each of them in perfect symmetry while watching cartoons.

Grandma brushed back Aiden's blonde curls to expose his bare forehead awaiting her kiss. He was dressed in a pair of baby blue pyjamas, complete with enclosed feet and a trap door. He giggled at Grandma's kisses and Rayne, in her nightgown of happy face emojis, much more suited to a seven-year-old, smiled.

It seemed as though having Grandma here and Grandma giving that 'piece of her mind' coupled with FACE protecting them sent a renewed sense of peace through their cozy home.

As the years passed and Rayne learned more about their neighbourhood, she came to understand that FACE was, as Grandma thought, an original tree from when the area was forest land. FACE stood about a kilometre from their home and a bit less than a kilometre on the other side of FACE was the main street that intersected the highway.

After that first day, Rayne spent hours playing under the watchful eye of FACE amid the other trees and shrubs along the path. It was the sacred place during the ebbs and flows of their family. When Mom and Dad were in a fighting phase, it was a place of escape. When Mom and Dad were in a stable phase, it was a place for adventure and wonderment.

What Rayne didn't realize though, in the throes of her playful harmony, was that the watchful eyes of FACE were always truly … watching.

. . .

DAD IS NEARBY. HE MAKES A NOISE LIKE A LAUGH AND IT STARTLES Rayne from FACE because Dad has not laughed in such a long time. Lately, Dad only cries. Rayne realizes as she returns to the whooshing breath, that the noise was not a laugh at all but an audible sob.

It used to be rare for Dad to cry. Rayne can only recall two other times. Once after Grandpa died when she and Aiden silently watched him from the back stairs. And another time, on family movie night, when he held Mom's hand while wiping his cheek as the movie score played a soulful violin.

Now Dad cries when he is near. Although it's usually just a murmur, it pierces louder than anyone else's. Rayne feels a tear escape her eyelid but then, because she cannot feel her face, wonders if it is running down her cheek.

The French man is here. He is pushing against her. He has brought the lady with the raspy voice. They are talking to Dad. Rayne can feel her tears for real now. They are warm and wet against her face as her stomach begins to churn. She wants FACE to come but it does not. The whooshing breath is louder now. She cries out and soon the French man is putting his arms beneath her shoulders. She feels like she is sitting up. The lady shouts but the words don't solidify. Rayne is horrifyingly dizzy and wants to vomit. A feeling from a day long ago is evoked and she cannot help but let it pull her back into her memory.

THAT DAY RAYNE SPUN AND SPUN AND THOUGHT THAT SHE MIGHT lose the cotton candy she had ingested. She heard Aiden laughing and looked over at his ten-year-old smile. It was his birthday and they had gone to ride the Devil's Spin. He was finally tall enough and the two sat side by side as the world rotated around them, faster and faster. Mom watched from the ground, her phone pointing up to them so she could video.

Rayne was embarrassed, afraid that Mom might video her being sick as Aiden laughed harder and harder. It wasn't just the cotton candy. Rayne was having cramps for only the second time in her life. She could not explain that to Aiden. She took a deep breath to hold in the cotton candy as the world swirled and the gagging feeling rose.

She knew she was going to be sick. It was beyond the point where your mind could convince your stomach. She turned away from her brother, feeling the burn, the release, the juxtaposition of relief and horror as her vomit erupted in swirls of beige and bright pink.

The only thing worse than the smell was the expressions on the other's faces as they spun by, trapped in their metal containers. A boy, about Aiden's age, pointed and laughed while two girls she recognized from last year's soccer matches gagged in disgust.

Rayne kept frozen with her back to Aiden for fear of another bout as she began to sob. The ride, oblivious to her suffering spun for two more rotations, finally slowing to the point where Aiden could safely move to reach her. She felt his hand on her back and as the noise subsided heard his soothing words.

Hours later, having escaped the amusement park and the cringing moment when Dad talked to the ride operator, Rayne left home to walk along the path to FACE. Leaning her back against FACE's cool bark she willed the energy to emit from the tree as she felt FACE's imaginary arms wrap her in safety. Hesitantly, she checked the phone she'd recently been given, awaiting the onslaught.

"Mom says dinner's in thirty minutes." Aiden startled her from behind. "If you want to eat."

She continued looking down at her phone awaiting the worst. Had those girls snapped a photo?

"Nobody saw." He kneeled next to her. "Nobody we know anyway."

Finding nothing in her feeds, she sighed in relief. "I guess."

"Even if they did," he continued. "Who cares? People puke! Are you feeling better?"

She nodded.

"That's good. I'm glad *I* didn't puke. I think I ate more cotton candy than you did. Plus, the pizza." He rubbed his stomach. "Mom made me a cake. Are you up for cake?"

"I'm not sure."

"Yeah, don't need you puking twice on my birthday. Don't need my birthday to be forever known as 'Rayne's Pukidy Puke Day'!"

She laughed and noticed he was staring up at FACE. A frown crept along Aiden's brow line.

"What?" She asked.

"Nothin'." He stood up and turned back to her. "So head back for dinner before Mom has to text you. You know how she gets." He turned quickly back to FACE, then headed down the path.

Rayne sat a moment longer, thankful her atrocious day would soon be a memory, thankful for her brother, and unaware that above her the corners of FACE's gaping mouth had turned downward into a frown.

NOW RAYNE KNOWS SHE IS GOING TO BE SICK AND CRIES ALOUD again as the French man shouts her name. How does he know who she is?

"Rayne, can you hear us?" The French man is pushing on her shoulder.

"Ray-bear? Ray-bear, it's Dad. Can you hear me?"

She doesn't want Dad here. Not Dad. She only wants FACE.

"Go ahead with the midazolam," the raspy-voiced lady speaks in a full sentence that Rayne almost understands.

In seconds the whooshing breath is gone and she is back in FACE's embrace. She stares at FACE's asymmetrical eyes and reaches out to touch the glistening red ladybug shells as they continue flowing downward.

"We'll go ahead with tomorrow." Mom's voice mixes with the whooshing breath. Rayne hears the words but they meander and hang alone without context. Is this the same day that Dad was here? Is it evening now?

"Are you one hundred percent sure?" Grandma's voice cuts into Rayne's thoughts. Grandma must have come to visit! "We could wait another week, you know. She'd want to be there."

"We shouldn't be talking about this here," Mom speaks so softly it's barely audible but Rayne is happy that, for once, she is understanding the words. "They've been weaning her off the drugs," Mom continues, "and I worry she can hear us."

Rayne feels her mother's fingers stroke the top of her hand.

"But I think they may be weaning her too fast. I guess this morning she got quite agitated and they had to give her more sedation."

"Okay, dear," Grandma begins. "We can talk outside but please reconsider. This is Aiden, after all. Rayne would want to be there."

Aiden? Rayne struggles to open her eyes but they won't cooperate. The heaviness of her lids is exemplified by a heaviness that overtakes her heart like a low thundercloud.

In these hours, days, weeks she has not heard Aiden's voice.

She squeezes her eyes tighter and wills an image of Aiden.

If only she could find FACE she could find Aiden. She could protect him like she always has.

. . .

AIDEN WAS ELEVEN AND, FOR NO REASON RAYNE COULD IMAGINE, the Downy boys at the end of the block decided he did not belong. He was other. They made his life a living hell of torment and despite teachers and guidance counsellors, Mom and Dad, and everything in Rayne's power, they were relentless. Rayne cried for her brother, knowing that her move to high school the year before eliminated her ability to watch over him.

That day, he arrived home with his nose bloody, his shoes damaged, and his bicycle dented. He tried his best to slip inside before she saw him, not realizing she was on her bike about to leave the garage.

"Dude!" Rayne stood at the garage door. She ran inside to grab a wet towel and dabbed at his face.

"I don't want Mom and Dad to know," he insisted as she continued cleaning him up. "Are they home?"

"Mom's inside. They have to know. I think it's broken."

"Not right now." He lowered his face to the ground and Rayne felt her heart break. He seemed thinner and paler than earlier in the summer. His nose continued to bleed as he dabbed it with the ever-reddening towel.

She nodded, staring at the dent on his bicycle. "Is it still riding okay?" She jumped back on her bike. "Come with me."

"Do you think it'll bruise?" Aiden asked a few minutes later as the two sat down across from each other in front of FACE.

"Yeah."

Aiden looked struck.

"Dude, it's a mess. They're going to find out and Mom will want you to go to the hospital," she added.

"I know. But they're fighting again." He stared down at the brush in front of FACE now worn like a carpet from their years of their devotion. "Now I'll be a new reason they fight."

"No, none of this is on you."

"I just feel alone." Aiden sighed.

"You're never alone. You've always got me." She leaned into FACE, pressing her head back to look up from below. "Whoa," she whispered, realizing FACE's eye was dropping further than before. She stood up to face the tree head-on as both of FACE's eyes had turned downward toward Aiden.

"What?"

"FACE. It looks like its eyes have moved."

"It's growing, I guess," Aiden said.

"I suppose." Rayne stepped back assessing the tree's new façade. It seemed as though FACE's mouth was now in a grimace.

Last night the French man shouted her name as the raspy-voiced lady prodded at her. Then came the elation. Rayne opened her eyes and saw them all, Mom, Dad and Grandma standing there amid a series of machines.

The French man, whose name is Daniel, wore pale blue scrubs that amplified his ginger hair. The raspy-voiced lady, Dr. Knowles, wore an emerald dress under a crisp, white coat. Her shiny, black hair was pulled in a low ponytail that made her face seem slim and kind.

Grandma cried so hard. She asked if anything hurt. Dr. Knowles shone bright lights in Rayne's eyes while Daniel asked her funny questions. How many fingers? When is her birthday? What is the name of her school?

Mom stroked Rayne's hair and told Rayne it had been eleven days since *the accident*. She wanted to know what Rayne remembered.

Rayne remembered nothing.

She wondered where Aiden was.

Now Rayne is back in the room remembering FACE's distorted expression and knowing in the deepest part of her soul that the ladybugs she continues to see flowing from FACE's eyes are not ladybugs at all.

Dad is mumbling and she feels the light touch of his hand on hers but she doesn't want him here.

"Ray-bear, can you hear me?"

Her heart hurts. It's not physical pain like when Daniel moves her body to keep her from getting sores. This is the nagging pain of angst that lives just below her throat.

She has not spoken much since last night. She whispered only a word or two to Grandma and the nurses. Hours after Daniel shouted her name, the medical team sedated her to pull a tube from the depths of her throat. It burnt like sandpaper, much worse than the simple sore throat of a cold.

"Ray-bear?" Dad is leaning in so far, that she can smell him. It is the pleasant smell of fresh laundry mixed with Dad's soap, the green bar soap that he has used for as long as she can remember. She closes her eyes and, for a moment, imagines the dad she used to know, her hero. She remembers him singing classic rock at the top of his lungs while driving and the concerned look he wore while carrying her home with a skinned knee.

The moment vanishes and she can only see the recent memory. The one she'd rather forget.

ANYA KELSEY. THE FIRST TIME RAYNE MET HER SHE WAS SITTING cross-legged on the living room sofa surrounded by turquoise paint chips. Mom had won a free decorating consultation as a door prize at a charity dinner. Rayne arrived home halfway through the chaos of Anya pointing to photos of window treatments, suggesting the removal of carpet to reveal natural wood, and a replacement of the kitchen floor. Anya had an intense way of speaking that seemed to bypass Mom as she made a small dig at the amount of clutter in the foyer.

Dad wasn't even home that night.

As Anya's newfound ideas for the living room, kitchen and foyer swelled into months and costs far beyond Mom and Dad's plans, it seemed to Rayne that Anya and Dad had never even met.

So, on the day that Rayne arrived home from school early due to a massive headache, she did not anticipate the scene before her. Knowing her parents were at work, she hadn't even tried to call them for a ride home and upon arrival, she'd expected the house to be empty.

Instead, Anya's silver BMW sparkled against the sunlight in front of the neighbour's house. Surprised that Anya would be there without Mom, Rayne assumed Anya must be doing work next door. Rayne proceeded through the house, past the now uncluttered foyer and through the gleaming, half-floored kitchen finding no one. She slipped up the staircase to head to her bedroom. Passing the loft that Dad sometimes used as an office, she paused, hearing a scuffling sound, and peered inside.

Dad, red-faced and grunting like an animal, leaned over the top of Anya, sprawled in ecstasy across Dad's desk. Rayne gasped, catching herself back into silence before they noticed. Looking away as shockwaves sent acid up her throat, Rayne turned to escape, only then noticing Anya's grey pencil skirt and black thong flung across the floor.

Unsure what to do as the pressure of her headache flooded forward, Rayne dashed up the second staircase to her room and quietly closed the door. For close to an hour she sat, wrapped in a thick afghan, praying for the sound of doors closing and cars starting. Finally, peering through the crack in her blinds, she saw Anya leave and a few minutes later, her father slipped back outside and away from the house, just moments before her mother arrived.

Rayne wondered if Dad knew she was there. Had he noticed her knapsack by the front door when he left? That first night, saved by her headache, Rayne remained in her room, wondering-- why? She said nothing, only observed his lies, her mother's naivety, and Anya's blatant deceits.

Rayne remembers this but she does not remember anything that came after. She does not remember what led her here to her bed in Highlands Hospital, 5th-floor rehab, other than some celebratory cheers this morning as Daniel and the other ICU staff waved goodbye while she stared at the moving ceiling.

"Ray-bear, Mom will be here soon," Dad says. He explains that Mom and Grandma will be back later and then they, along with Emily will meet. Emily has already been by once. She is a beautiful woman with a Jamaican accent and thick, black hair. She is a therapist who asks a lot of questions but gives no answers. Something in Emily's eyes makes Rayne anxious, as though she is evaluating Rayne's reactions and anticipating disaster.

"Honey, is there any way we can talk before the others come?" Dad asks and Rayne feigns sleep.

RAYNE REACHES TO TOUCH FACE AND THIS TIME HER HAND FEELS it. The crimson flood of ladybugs is sticky and moist against her trembling fingers. Then, FACE is gone and Rayne is awake again, back in her hospital room.

Emily's hand on her shoulder feels intrusive despite her being kind and gentle. A nurse whose name Rayne can't recall is standing beside her with a cup containing two tablets and a glass of water. Mom, Dad and Grandma have taken turns explaining the past week, as though they had rehearsed the dialogue over and over.

It seems they are telling the story backwards starting with Rayne waking up yesterday.

No one has said the words: Aiden is dead. But Rayne already knows that.

The day before yesterday they buried Aiden in the cemetery next to Grandpa, they explain. Before that, there was a funeral attended by everyone he knew. *Almost everyone.* They wanted to wait for her to come but were unsure if she would ever awaken. Mom's voice quivers when she says this.

Despite tears and hesitations, the funeral descriptions come relatively easily and matter-of-factly. It is the next part of the backward timeline where the story distorts. Dad reaches for Mom's hand as Rayne feels bile twist up her throat and the words form in snippets of realization. She pictures each letter jumbling together like creative movie credits in an awkward font.

"Accident."

"Car accident."

"Right at the intersection."

She wants FACE.

She squeezes her eyes tightly shut. *No. No. No.*

"Don't blame yourself," Grandma pleads.

"Do you remember anything at all?" Emily asks.

Rayne can't breathe.

"It's too much," Mom nods to the nurse who offers the tablets. "Take these and rest and we'll talk more in a while."

Rayne pops the tablets under her tongue as instructed. Their voices go softer, like a TV playing in another room. She slides into a hypnotized haze.

FACE has two eyes. They are symmetrical. Both eyes are pushed back like stepped-on soda cans. They are watching her in petrified stillness. There is no nose, only chiselled skin in checker box rows that crawl with …

They are not ladybugs at all.

They are the crimson flow of blood.

The mouth laughs.

And, for the first time, she can smell it.

It's the smell of nature, of being outside. She is lying against the tree amid the mucky mud trail. Next to her, Aiden's crushed skull and broken body lie amid the twisted metal and broken glass of Dad's SUV.

R AYNE GUESSES IT IS EVENING. F ROM HER HOSPITAL BED, SHE CAN see the lights in the parking structure across the street. At her request, Mom has left Rayne's phone charging on the bedside table. It is the first time she has had it in a long time. Rayne lifts it and feels the smooth façade. Unlocking it with her thumb she stares down at the hundreds of messages. Bypassing them, she Googles the story published on that day.

"Tragic and Mysterious Accident leaves One Dead, another clinging to Life"

At the top of the article, Aiden smiles. He is in the striped soccer shirt he wore in last year's tournament. His shaggy hair cascades in front of his face, blocking one of his deep blue eyes.

The story is kind-hearted. Beloved. Unthinkable. *'The fourteen-year-old is dead and his seventeen-year-old sister, the driver, is fighting for her life. The girl was speeding…'*

A sob escapes her throat and she closes her eyes for a moment to block the words.

'The girl was speeding when she lost control and ended up facing oncoming traffic resulting in the SUV swerving to avoid a van. The SUV then careened over the shoulder into a tree.'

Below the photo of Aiden is a photo of the gnarled SUV.

'into a tree'

She clicks it to expand the photo then spreads her fingers to zoom on the tree.

The mouth has a lopsided gape …

No. A grin.

From the hallway outside, a metal cart with a wonky wheel makes its way down the corridor.

Soon an elderly woman in a purple smock appears holding a glass of water. She reaches to pass it to Rayne's bedside table but misjudges as water, ice cubes and a small vase of flowers crash to the tile floor.

"Oh, oh my dear. I'm so sorry," the volunteer exclaims. "Let me get something to clean that up."

Rayne stares at the mess of stems and ice on the floor as her memories return to a similar mess of a shattered dinner plate on the new kitchen floor.

"WHAT THE HELL IS WRONG WITH YOU, RAYNE!" MOM JUMPED FROM the kitchen table and tripped across the peas, scattered in multiple directions amid cauliflower chunks before rushing to the broom closet next to the kitchen.

"What's wrong with me? Jesus!" Rayne stood, hands on hips. "Are you really that blind, Mom?"

"Apparently I am!" Mom yelled from across the room. "You've been miserable for weeks and now this, a temper tantrum at dinner. What are you, two?"

"Calm down," Dad said. "Both of you calm down. I don't know what's gotten into you this past while, Rayne."

Aiden sipped water, red-faced and pleading with his eyes for Rayne to sit.

"Oh my God!" Rayne walked toward the counter. "Seriously, Dad. Seriously, you and Mom are fighting, AGAIN, about the cost of the home renovations. Fighting AGAIN about this God damned floor." She kicked the floor with her heel. "There's more important things going on in the world and in this house, you know! And besides, the whole damn thing should be free."

"Ali, stop. Stop cleaning up her mess!" Dad yelled at Mom who returned with a dustpan.

"What should be free?" Mom turned to Rayne.

"These renovations. Tell her, Dad," Rayne challenged. "Tell her." She sent daggers to her father's eyes and, in an instant, there was a realization.

"Rayne," he hesitated but shook his head.

"Tell me what?"

"I'm out of here!" Rayne kicked the counter and reached into the basket for her father's car keys.

"Ask Anya."

"What about Anya?" Mom yelled.

"What are you doing? You aren't taking my car!" Dad rose and grabbed Rayne's wrist. She wrestled free, stormed out the front door and beelined it for her father's SUV.

"Rayne?" Aiden ran from the door toward her. "Rayne, what's going on?"

"Get in."

"What?"

"Get in, Aiden." She waited as he rushed to the passenger door and she peeled out the driveway, her father's face appearing in the front door window.

Weeks have passed but the minutes, hours and days are a blur. Rayne stays in her room thinking only of Aiden.

The truth, now as exposed as their half-torn-apart house, takes up more space than Rayne can bear. Grandma has gone back home again. She was feeling 'in the way' and lost to understand her son. Dad is living here, but sleeping in the guest room. Mom is quiet and it is impossible to tell for whom or what she is mourning from one moment to the next.

Friends dropped over but gradually that has stopped. They offered prayers and hopes and recommendations but all have been ignored like a tall pile of mail.

Yesterday, after much begging, Dad took Rayne to the accident scene. She left him sitting in his new car on the nearest dirt road and walked to the tree.

The lush greens from the day of the accident have turned a burnt October orange. The authorities have cleared all remnants of Dad's car, of Aiden.

FACE's curvy leaves are the brown of light chocolate.

"Why?" She reaches her hand against FACE and is drawn in. She places her ear against the rough bark and listens.

MONTHS HAVE PASSED AND A LIGHT DUST OF SNOW SHIMMERS across the road. Today Rayne is calmer than she has felt in ages. She pulls Mom's car toward the dirt road again and parks. Grabbing her knapsack, she walks toward FACE.

Now barren of leaves, the lopsided mouth seethes. She leans once again to feel the coldness of the bark against her cheek and understands. She can smell the dampness. She longs for it.

With the soul of her boot, she lifts herself onto the first notch, then climbs like a child up the main trunk and bottom branches, finally reaching the high horizontal branch she's longed for.

She reaches into her bag and pulls out the rope.

- ❧ -

ABOUT K. BRADLEY

K. Bradley (formerly Kathi Nidd) is the author of the mystery thrillers *Claire, departed* (2024) and *Snowdrifts* (2016). She is currently working toward the publication of two additional mystery thrillers set in the same fictional city as part of the "Millerton Mysteries."

Her poetry has appeared in publications by The Poetry Institute of Canada, Polar Expressions Publishing, Haunted Waters Press and Quills Magazine. As the creator of "Fuzzball's Christmas Eve Adventure" and its sequel "Fuzzball's Enormously Big Little Brother", Bradley engages adults and children alike with 100% of the profit to animal shelters. Most recently her short story works were included in publications by the Kanata Fiction Circle: "Seven Deadly Pens" and "A Write Christmas."

With a career in healthcare informatics, Bradley pulls from the human side of medicine to provide a unique lens into strong and realistic characters. She grew up and continues to reside in Ottawa alongside her loving spouse, a spirited mini schnauzer, and a pensive pug.

Read more at www.writingspot.ca or contact Kathi at askthewritingspot@gmail.ca.

Facebook: https://www.facebook.com/WritingSpot

A
GOOD
MAN
MATT C. SULLY

A GOOD MAN

MATT C. SULLY

William Powell slipped off his wedding band and wiped his palms. The old Zippo shifted in his pants with each pass, clicking open and shut like a pocket lint Pacman. He had successfully quit smoking years ago. Even in prison, when the night air was thick with contraband clouds, he hadn't reverted into the habit. He had promised his wife.

Scientists claimed the urge to start smoking, like other addictions, was genetically predetermined. Was quitting any different? Were both actions something *he* had actually decided to do or were they preset milestones on a life path laid out for him? No forks in the road. No scenic route. Just a beginning leading to an end.

William gripped the wheel and slowed the delivery van. He took a deep breath to calm his nerves, but it set off a coughing fit. The piña colada air freshener twirled in the mini gusts, a better wind vane than a deodorizer. The cabin smelled like sweat and icing sugar, and the fumes of the jerry cans had begun to seep in from the back.

Signs ahead marked directions and names of company buildings, though he didn't bother reading them. The InnoSeq Genomics campus was sprawling and vast, spread across fifty private acres, but there were only three main buildings. William assumed they were leaving room for expansion.

From the perfectly smooth roads and manicured hedges to the abstract sculptures positioned between sleek architectural designs of glass and curved steel, the allegedly illustrious company's secluded lands had the air of a modern billionaire's estate—new money.

At the first crossroads, the van turned left. William assisted the wheel, unable to abandon the idea that he wasn't in full control, although he struggled to remember the last time he was.

William Powell knew he was no mastermind. If he had any technical ability, he would have tried hacking into the network from the outside. If he had money or the right connections, he would have hired someone more qualified to break in. Instead, he was on his own, relying on timing and a basic sense of trust.

The trust was that a delivery man was just a delivery man. The van he stole, his only major intentional crime to date, was a legitimate UPS vehicle. William's brown shirt and pants matched the theme. The timing was the day itself: Christmas on a Saturday, a union of events he hoped meant InnoSeq staff would be nonexistent and security would be at a minimum.

The gatehouse guard helped prove William right. The man was prepared to let him pass even before William offered him homemade sugar cookies. If the men inside were as lax or as hungry, he'd be hitting the highway before anyone could pull the fire alarm.

The van pulled into a visitor space, the electric whir abruptly cutting out. William was relieved to see the parking lot was empty, but the silence outside was eerie. He glanced through the doors of the building's main entrance. A guard watched him from behind a high desk, stoically staring through tinted glasses as William stepped out the van's side opening.

Raising the sliding door in back, William pretended to check for the right packages. One of his boxes had sprung a leak. Its label had begun to peel away, likely from the gas's toxic fumes. He pressed down the corners but they curled up each time he took away his fingers. Sweat dripped down the back of his neck.

"Relax," he whispered to himself, sliding the ruined box to the side. He had others.

He lifted a dry box into his arms and moved toward the entrance. The guard met him there, but made no move to open the doors. The guard pressed a button mounted on the frame. His voice came through a speaker on the opposite side.

"Who are you?"

William knew the truck's logo was visible, as was the patch on his shirt he'd so carefully sewn. And then there was the package in his hands. Perhaps he had mistaken stoic for stupid.

He offered the same grin he'd shown to the gatehouse guard. "Santa Claus."

The guard's lenses had darkened even more in the direct light. William could hardly see the man's eyes, a chilling effect he was certain was intentional. His mustache was bushy, though it remained a flat line of indifference. Tinged yellow near his lips, the mark of a heavy smoker, William was tempted to bum a square.

"We're not expecting a delivery," said the guard.

"An unexpected delivery is called a gift." William tried another smile and received the same flat response.

"Look, Santa. That line may have worked on Spencer out front, but I plan on keeping my job."

"Letting a delivery van through is grounds for dismissal?"

"With the proper confirmation, no, but he didn't radio me a

heads up and, just before you parked, I saw him fall asleep. He's lazy. The boss won't tolerate it."

"It's Christmas."

"We still have a job to do."

"And so do I. Are you taking this package or do you want me to climb down the chimney?"

"Leave it outside."

So much for trust.

William huffed and shifted the box in his arms. The weight was beginning to strain his back. "You're really not letting me in?"

The guard shook his head. The plan had met its end before it had begun. He needed to get the jerry cans inside; the fire wouldn't do much from the exterior. William set the package on the ground and went back to the van.

William didn't know what else to do but fetch package after package. His only hope was the guard would see how many there were and want help bringing them inside, but he just stood there and watched him work. William put the wet box behind the others. Appearances mattered little now.

"Well," said William, legitimately winded, "last one."

The guard leaned over and pressed the speaker button. "You're forgetting something."

A signature. He could have asked for a signature. "Yes. Let me grab my machine."

"No. I never sign. I want one of those cookies."

This time William tried *not* to smile. "Cookies?"

"The ones I saw you give Spencer."

"You saw that?"

The guard pushed his glasses down his nose. His brown eyes were kind of lovely, not intimidating at all. Keeping them hidden was a strategic ploy. He wouldn't want anyone mistaking him as kind.

"I see everything."

"Yeah." William rolled his eyes. "Okay."

He trotted back to the van and returned with a tin of home-made cookies, the same ones he had given the gatehouse guard, the same ones he'd tainted with a generous number of sleeping pills. He dropped the tin on top of the boxes.

"Take the rest. I've got more at home."

"Thanks. I skipped breakfast and I'm starving."

Trust and timing.

"No problem."

William drove back to the gatehouse and took the snoozing guard's access key and gun. When he returned to the main building, Ebenezer Stooge was hunched over his desk dreaming of sugar plums. William confiscated his gun.

He stole his cigarettes too.

THE LOBBY OF INNOSEQ GENOMICS' MAIN BUILDING HOUSED A slender pine tree with a single strand of silver garland. It was the artsy, non-committal version of Christmas, but the boxes which had concealed William's jerry cans countered the minimal festive imagery.

They were torn and scattered just like every present in thousands of households across the country. Shredded copies of *Genomics America* stuffing dotted the space like spent party poppers. The only thing missing were sleepy-eyed parents and giddy children.

William should have been living the suburban life with his own kids, but he was no longer welcome at home. He was out playing Santa instead, only in lieu of holiday cheer, William was spreading gasoline.

He had hauled the guard safely around the side of the build-ing, another art piece for the landscape: 'Dickhead in Glasses.'

Both guards' weapons he had stuffed into a nearby manicured bush. With no alarms and no more watchful eyes, William now took his time distributing the fuel in connected pools. The halls glistened and the fumes were bringing him to a euphoric joy.

William readied his new key card in one hand, his old lighter in the other. He had them raised like trophies over the impending bonfire when he heard a familiar whirring from outside.

A golf-cart-sized vehicle skidded to a stop near the delivery van. A massive, uniformed man grazed his head on its roof as he exited. He and William briefly connected eyes. The big guard scanned William before darting his gaze to the empty front desk.

The guard clutched his radio. A second radio behind the desk amplified his voice. William jumped.

"Deckard. Where are you?"

William slowly backed from the door, stuffing the key card and Zippo into his shirt pocket. Like Deckard, this guy kept his target in his sights, an awareness William had failed to maintain. He should have been more diligent in taking a head count. He should have studied harder in prison.

"Deckard had mentioned Spencer's name," William said to himself. "He also mentioned a boss."

Gas began to soak into William's shoes. He had been careful to avoid it before, but he was moving backward now, not watching where he was going. William moved behind the desk, shoes squishing out new pools, and picked up Deckard's radio. He lifted the device to his mouth, but the Boss spoke first.

"Who are you?"

The Santa bit had run its course. "A dissatisfied customer."

"Are those gas canisters?"

"It's not safe here. You should go."

The Boss released his radio and leaned into the vehicle, retrieving a large baton and a gun.

William shook his head. "He's not gonna go."

He turned and ran, shoes squeaking and slipping. As he rounded the first corner, the panel at the front door beeped. He heard the doors open with a mighty whoosh. An alarm sounded moments later, red lights flashing overhead as William dashed down the empty halls, taupe walls and doors marked with small plaques he had no time to read. The signs he was following were higher up and pointed to the only door he wanted to find.

William turned down two more corridors before he spotted the emergency exit and a woman in a lab coat making a desperate attempt to open it. She slid her key card furiously across the nearby sensor, pumping the door's stretched handle with every beep. She resembled an old rail line inspector working a hand cart, only she wasn't going anywhere. The lock wouldn't release.

The menacing cadence of large boots striking porcelain echoed down the halls behind him. The hairs down the back of William's neck prickled, yet he was frozen with indecision. He wasn't the only rat trapped in the maze.

The woman turned. Spotting William, his dull delivery uniform splashed in siren red, she morphed from startled to perplexed, but their realizations were one. The traditional way out was no longer an option. She side-eyed the only open door in the hallway. White light spilled from within like a heavenly beckoning. When she started for it, William followed.

His sprint was clunky and desperate, but William's shoes were sturdy. He jammed one into the gap of the closing door and shoved his way into the room behind the woman. She stumbled back, flailing, lab coat rippling like a hero's cape. William mule-kicked the door and grabbed her, pinning her to the wall.

The alarm continued to echo in and around them, but the big man's thunderous footfalls had gone silent. William slid his hand over the woman's mouth. She was trembling, a syncopated partner to the pounding rhythm of William's heart. Her heated breath passed over his fingers. His heavy wheezes swirled her auburn hair. She wriggled against the incongruous coupling, but couldn't break free. Chased into hiding and unable to move, all either of them could do was wait.

He whispered in her ear. "Don't you dare scream."

THE BOSS CALLED OUT FROM THE HALLWAY, THOUGH IT WASN'T FOR William or the woman. He was shouting for the other guards. Repeatedly, he called for Deckard and Spencer over his radio. Neither man responded, nor would they, and not just because they were vacationing in Dreamland. William had taken their radios too. He reached into his pocket and turned the volume low on Deckard's stolen unit.

Voice progressively more frustrated and furious, the Boss eventually quit hailing his men. Shortly after, the Doppler rise and fall of the Boss' stalking run signaled his exit from the hall. William relaxed his hold on the woman and eased away by inches to reveal her face.

She was young, maybe just breaking twenty-five, and her green eyes were watered and red. William's heart sank. He lowered his hand from her mouth and stepped back. Her hands went up as if she were miming a wall closing in.

"I can explain," she said.

William was puzzled. He looked around the room for whatever he may have missed. The space was a series of long counters and workstations, computers alongside machinery William didn't recognize and scientific standards of vials and beakers whose names he hadn't known since high school. The walls and floors were bright white, almost blindingly so.

"What?" he asked.

With distance between them and the clear light of the lab, the woman scanned William's uniform, stopping at his chest and the UPS patch stitched onto it.

"You're not with security?" she asked. "You're a *delivery* man?"

"I'm neither, actually."

"*You're* the reason for the alarm!?"

"Yeah. I'm sorry for scaring you. I didn't come here to hurt anyone."

She looked him over again. "Why are you here then?"

"To bring this place down."

She snorted, as if the notion were ridiculous. She came away from the wall, straightening her twisted blouse and ruffled lab coat, making clear her agitation. The name badge on her coat read 'D. Goodwin.'

"Well, whatever your plan is," she said, "I don't think it's working."

"No shit."

Goodwin shook her head. "You need to leave."

"I'd love to." He fished the guard's keycard from his pocket and held it up. "Is this thing going to work?"

"I doubt it. Mine wouldn't and I have campus-wide access."

"Crap." He stuffed the card back into his pants. "Then how do I get out?"

"In handcuffs, if you're lucky."

"That's not an option."

"The front desk might have an override for the doors, but you'd have to deal with the guard."

"The desk guard is gone. The only one left is the big guy."

"Gone? What did you do?"

"Nothing. Let's go."

Goodwin walked to a nearby workspace, its surface dominated by computer hardware and a lone sheet of paper. "I'm not going anywhere."

The computer screens were aglow with a company portal open on one, a file folder open on another. The final screen was filled with a slow-scrolling DNA sequence. He had done so much reading on the subject that he recognized the pattern instantly. She dropped into a rolling chair, back against the desk.

"I have work to do," said Goodwin. "You made your way in. Now make your way out."

She was beginning to make him angry. "If you don't go, you're going to get hurt."

"By you?"

"Not directly, but yes, and I don't want anyone to get hurt."

"You said that, right after you were done shoving me against a wall."

"My beef is with InnoSeq, not you. This company needs to be stopped." William's cheeks were warm.

"Look, delivery guy. However you feel you've been wronged, you can't just stop a company like InnoSeq, nor should you. The work we've done has led to dozens of medical breakthroughs, identified early markers for disease, mental disorders, and improved millions of lives."

"Not all lives are improved by your work."

"So that's why you're here. You're upset about something revealed in your SnapMap."

"SnapMap. Ridiculous name."

"It's marketing. Not my department, and probably not the name I'd have chosen if it was, but the science is sound."

"You're labeling people by their DNA as if that's all a person is."

"DNA *is* what a person is." She pulled her lab coat taut and folded her hands in her lap. He was something to observe now, a subject. "Acknowledging that is a good thing," she continued. "It helps us address issues early. Sometimes it's embarrassing, but whatever your issue is, there's no need to be angry. There are psychiatrists and medicine that can help you."

"That's what this is all about. Medicine and money, and no, DNA is not what a person is."

"I think you're failing to understand the science."

"I understand enough. The genetic markers, how their arrangement and combination can determine a person *possibly* developing a disease or whatever, but you're presenting it as fact, and it's not. You're nothing but psychics with crystal balls pretending you can accurately predict the future. You don't understand people, not who they are and certainly not who they'll become."

"It's true. No science is 100 percent, but our accuracy holds at 99.99."

"Which means .01 percent of the time, you're wrong, and with over 9 billion people on our earth, that's hundreds of thousands of false positives."

"No, it's not." Goodwin squirmed. "I've been here 3 years. You know what my job is? Correcting false readings. You know how many of those .01 erroneous readings are because of tainted samples? Almost every damned one. The program works. It just does."

"But some have to be wrong or you wouldn't have a job."

Goodwin looked away. "Yeah, maybe. Regardless, the likelihood of your readout being wrong is extremely low. You can ask for another analysis or give a new sample, but you knew there could be unfavorable discoveries. It's what you agreed to."

"I didn't agree to give InnoSeq any sample, and I didn't ask to have my DNA analyzed."

"I don't understand."

"What's hard to understand? You read my DNA without my permission and made all my *unfavorable discoveries* public information!"

Goodwin furrowed her brow. "We don't do that."

"The scientific journal that published that damned story sure did!"

"Scientific journal?" Goodwin's shoulders slumped. "Oh. *Genomics America.* I remember that article. The research group was studying genetic markers on felons. Violent offenders. You were one of them?"

"Yeah, and my lawyer and I fought to have those charges stricken from my record. I got out of prison and was carrying on with my life. I was in a good place finally, then that article came out and screwed it all up! Now I can't get a job. My friends have stopped talking to me, and my wife and sons…. "

"I'm sorry for your situation, but that wasn't our doing. That research group should never have publicized your names. InnoSeq doesn't even *keep* PII. We analyze the samples and give them a unique DNA ID and that's the information the client matches up on their end. We issue the results. They put names to it. We understand how sensitive that data is to the public."

"You just don't want the responsibility for what you do."

"We respect your privacy."

"You respect your profits."

"Every company does, but I know what you mean." Goodwin sighed. "Profit shouldn't be the only concern."

The alarms announcing William's intrusion ceased cycling through their grating peaks and valleys. William stood from the wall and peered out the door. The hallway no longer resembled a night club. The lights had returned to their mundane glow. He gingerly closed the door and turned back to Goodwin.

"Think they gave up?" he asked.

"I doubt it, but the exit might be open now."

"Maybe, but I'm not leaving. Not yet. Not until I see my file."

"What?"

He neared Goodwin's desk and glanced at the screens and

the single piece of paper. It was severely creased as if it had been folded over multiple times. On it there were two columns, one for names, and one for a long series of numbers.

"Bring up my file. William Powell. P-O-W—"

"That's not how it works. Like I said, I can't just look up your name in our system."

"Then what do you need?"

"Well, I need your DNA."

William took the guard's keycard from his pocket and snapped it in half. He doubted it would open any doors, but it could still open a vein. He held out his hand.

"You got something to take this?"

"Take what?"

"My blood."

WILLIAM POWELL SLICED HIS PINKY LENGTHWISE, BLOOD TRICKLING from the wound. Goodwin cursed and reached for a nearby vial. William brought his hand to it and a red trail oozed down the vial's long neck.

"We don't need this much."

She pulled the vial away. William removed his brown shirt and wrapped his hand. His lighter fell to the floor with a jarring series of clinks. He scooped it up and set it on the desk. Goodwin navigated a menu system in the company portal and a drawer opened in a small metal box beside the monitors. She inserted the vial and closed the drawer.

After more menu clicks and keyboard clacks, the monitor with the DNA sequence went black. A new sequence began moving across the void. They both stared, waiting. Outside, somewhere in the empty hallway, a beep sounded and a door opened. The Boss was checking behind each one. He hadn't given up.

William leaned in close, squeezing the desk and the back of Goodwin's chair. Her hair tickled his chest.

"You smell," she said.

"Sorry. I've worked up a sweat."

"It's more than B.O. You smell like gasoline. Might want a shower before you light up again."

"Sorry." William clutched the Zippo and slid it into his pocket with Deckard's cigarettes. "Don't worry about me. I quit."

Goodwin dismissed him. "Sure."

William backed off a few inches, but kept his eyes affixed to the screen.

"You already know what we're going to find," said Goodwin. "It's not going to change."

"But it is, because you're going to change it."

The young woman turned, eyes narrowed. "I can't do that."

"You already told me you can."

"Well I won't! So your DNA markers will show a genetic propensity for violence. A lot of people have that and employers are often lenient. With your record cleared, you should be fine, as long as they don't read scientific journals."

"It's more than the assault."

There was another beep. Another door. William was scared. Then the second screen flashed: "Match Found."

She was right. There was no name, just a unique DNA ID and a long list of Single-Nucleotide Polymorphisms, or SNPs. Together they formed his DNA SNP Map.

His map was compiled and translated into simple keywords, labels about the human they formed at a genetic level. He had read it before, but scanned it again, hoping it had already somehow changed: "Smoking; High Cholesterol; Depression; Liver Cancer; etc."

A special section outlined in red was reserved for "Common

Good" findings. "Violent Tendencies" was high on the list, though it was not at the top. William stood back in anticipation as Goodwin perused his file. She spun in her chair, eyes wide. For the first time he saw real fear in them.

"Murder?"

"It's not true. I've never murdered anyone." William put up his hands. Blood had soaked through his shirt and dripped onto the floor. "I swear to you I have not and never will murder anyone."

"Yeah? And you say you're not a smoker either yet you carry a lighter, and I've heard the rattle in your lungs."

"I told you I quit."

There was another door beep. It sounded close.

"Your markers are facts, proven ones." She put out her fingers to begin a count. "You smoke."

"I quit!" he shouted.

Goodwin winced. She waited a moment before continuing, her voice much softer. "And you have a history of violence."

Another door shut. Beep. Another opened. Then the radio in William's pocket crackled. He took it out, leaving the volume low.

"I can hear you shouting," said the Boss. "I'll find you soon," William and Goodwin's eyes were locked, "and I'm going to kill you for what you did to my men."

Goodwin's eyes watered. "You *are* a killer, aren't you Powell?"

"Those guards are fine." He tried to sound calm. He tried to sound comforting. He was confident he failed at both. "I drugged them with sleeping pills. That's all. I don't want to hurt anyone. I never did."

"Liar."

A nearby beep. William thought he felt air spill into the lab, though their door remained shut. He moved quickly toward the desk and gripped the arms of Goodwin's chair. The blood from his pinky's makeshift dressing had become tacky, and the pain from the wound was like lightning shooting up his arm.

"Do you know why I got that assault charge?"

She leaned back, shaking her head. "You know I don't."

"Because one day I stopped into the store for smokes and when I came out I saw a man shouting at my wife. They were arguing over a parking space. This was back when we parked our own cars. He claimed it was his. She claimed it was ours. I could have been okay with the idiot's shouting, but then he touched her.

"Maybe I didn't need to punch him. I was younger then, hotheaded, and yes, I took it too far. I wanted to kill him for touching her. I'll admit that killing him even crossed my mind, but I didn't do it.

"Back someone into a corner or threaten someone or something they love and people, not just me, but *all* people can be driven to kill. I recognized what I was capable of that day and I made a choice. I made a choice to hurt that man, but I didn't kill him. Whatever my genetics want me to be, I'm more than my DNA. I'm a good man and I love my family."

"If you're such a family man, why are you here terrorizing people instead of spending Christmas with your wife and kids?"

Tears filed down William's cheeks. "Because they won't see me. My boys, I think, are just confused by the situation, but my wife…. After the assault, you know, she supported me. When I was in prison, she drove an hour both ways to see me, as often as she could. She made sure I knew she loved me, that she wasn't angry for what I did. Hell, she was proud of me, proud that her husband stood up and protected her. I was her hero.

"But then the article, the test, they went public. It wasn't until you put that label on me that she started to look at me different, like the way you're looking at me now. She's terrified of me, terrified that she doesn't know me. And I'm terrified of losing her."

Heavy footfalls caught William and Goodwin's attention. The Boss was just outside the lab door.

"Please," William said, rounding a long lab table that divided the room. "If I go back to prison, I may never see them again. I just want my life back, Goodwin." William crouched out of sight and whispered, "Please."

He slunk into the limited shadows, balling himself up, pulling his knees into his chest, his back to a cabinet beneath the table. He could no longer see Goodwin and there was nowhere left to run. William closed his eyes and listened. After a long beep, the door opened with force.

"Oh!" There was a cacophony of sounds William couldn't identify. It could have been Goodwin backing her chair into the desk or the door hitting the wall, but there was a rustling too, possibly a gun being drawn from its holster. "Miss Goodwin. I didn't realize you were here."

The quiet was long and terrifying.

"Oh. I must have forgotten to check in."

Fresh tears cooled William's face. She wasn't going to rat him out after all.

"Forgotten? Deckard doesn't allow anyone to forget, Miss Goodwin."

"Well, I came in the back."

"You're not supposed to do that, and no one is supposed to be in today."

William could feel the conversation's tension permeating, but he didn't understand what Goodwin was saying. Was she nervous and just saying nonsense or was something else going on? William envisioned her gesturing toward William's hiding spot, signaling the Boss to attack.

"Was that why the alarms went off?" asked Goodwin.

"No, ma'am. I don't want to concern you, but a man entered the building without authorization."

"Oh? Is he violent? I mean, has anyone been hurt?"

"No. Not hurt. Just a little groggy. When the alarm sounded, why didn't you—" the Boss paused. "Is that blood?"

From behind the table, William's eyes popped open. He looked at the shirt wrapped around his hand. Though the bleeding appeared to have slowed, it had spread in winding blotches. The delivery uniform was a mess, one which had apparently not been contained.

"Oh. Yeah. I dropped a sample," said Goodwin. "I'll clean it up later."

"I don't want to tell you your business, Miss Goodwin, but you should be more careful. These things are important, wouldn't you say?"

"Yes. You're right, Mister Bannion. In some capacity, we're handling people's lives."

William whispered the name. "Bannion."

"Right. Well, stay put for now. You'll be alright?"

"I think so."

"Good. I have to go catch this son of a bitch. When that is done, I want to see you in my office."

"What? Why?"

"To discuss your disregard for security and what reasoning you have for being here today."

"I have work to do!"

"On Christmas? Alone? Actually…"

William heard footsteps cross the room. He tensed, waiting to be discovered, but Goodwin's objections told him that *she* was the one under attack. William listened to the chaotic movements of people in a scuffle. He unraveled his soiled shirt and balled his fists. The cut pinky throbbed. His anger swelled with every pump of his heart.

"What are you doing?" she snapped. Her tone was heightened but not yet desperate.

"Taking your keycard and badge," said Bannion, matter of factly.

William leaned to his side, sliding his feet out in readiness to lunge from hiding, but Goodwin didn't shout for help. From the sounds of it, she never even rose from her chair. Bannion's clops and the door clicking open indicated the fight was over, but William couldn't relax.

Bannion had riled him up, but it was Goodwin that had gotten under his skin. William closed his eyes again and replayed the past half hour in his mind, highlighting details he'd missed the original go round. When he first saw Goodwin, she had run from him, then said she thought he was security. Why run from your own company's security?

"Don't leave this room," said Bannion.

He sounded dubious that his instruction would be heeded, and rightly so. The young woman scientist was acting damned suspicious. The door closed and Goodwin sounded the all clear.

"He's gone," she said.

William emerged from the long table, supporting himself on the cold surface top as he stretched his back and flexed his injured hand.

Goodwin was wiping her hands on her coat. "You told the truth about the guards. It's the only reason I didn't send you packing."

"Really?" he asked. "I think there's another reason you didn't want that guard finding me in your lab. I've told you why I came here on Christmas. I think it's time you tell me why *you're* here."

She turned back to the computer and worked the menu system and hit enter on the keyboard. A red-lined SNP disappeared from William's list.

"Did you just fix my file?"

"I changed it," said Goodwin. "There was nothing to fix, because nothing was broken."

She took the paper with the list of names and spread it in front of her keyboard. She began entering a long series of numbers, bringing up another file.

"But you removed the 'murder' label from my map?"

"Yes."

"And you're changing those too?"

He watched the DNA file stretch across the screen and the profile build. The SNP labels were few. The special red-lined section was blank, that is until Goodwin started adding to it: 'Violent Tendencies, Rape, Pedophilia."

William leaned over to read some of the names. He thought he even recognized a few. "You said you didn't have names. You also said the program was always right. What are you doing?"

Goodwin kept working as she spoke. She updated one file and moved on to another. Her fingers tapped out the numbers with frantic speed.

"The program *does* work, which is why when they asked me to start correcting false readings for samples that were untainted, I checked for justification. When I found there was none, you know what they told me?"

William was working on a response when Goodwin decided there was no need for one.

"They told me to stop checking," she said. "'The science is moving fast,' they said. 'Just make the changes,' they said. I reluctantly obliged, partly because there were so few, but some colleagues of mine were unhappy about the circumstances." She added more labels to a new nearly pristine profile, then closed it to make way for the next. "And then the number of change requests started growing and they were always for removing labels, never adding."

"You don't think they were false readings."

"I *know* they weren't, but I couldn't understand why. Then, last week at the company Christmas party we began piecing it together. That room was filled with investors and top donors, and we realized there had been a pattern. For every big donation that was announced for the company throughout the year, I received a request to update a false reading."

"The rich were paying to have their records cleaned."

"And I'm making them dirty again." She hit enter with a flourish and crumpled the list of donors.

"What will that do?"

"A whole lot of nothing, most likely. Even if I make the list public or reveal the true profiles for these bastards, they'll just blame a crazed employee for the snafu. I only came here today to verify our suspicions, not sabotage the company. Unlike you, I have no intention of 'bringing this place down.'"

"Then why do any of this? Why help me?"

"Because I think my career at InnoSeq Genomics might have reached an end today thanks to you, so I'm being petty. I still trust the science, but I no longer trust the people. If I had more time, maybe my colleagues and I could root out the corruption. I know your own circumstances haven't benefited from our work, but many have, and I'd hate to see good science fail."

Trust and timing.

"I understand, and I appreciate your help." William gripped her shoulder and squeezed. "Really. Thank you."

He parted from the young woman scientist and opened the lab door, slipping into the empty corridor. Goodwin followed.

"What are you doing?" he asked.

"With what happened, I can guarantee an investigation, and just me being here today without their knowledge is reason enough for termination. At best Bannion will have me fired. Worst case scenario, you and I both go to prison."

"We could run to Bolivia like Butch and Sundance." William flashed a counterfeit smile.

Goodwin shook her head. "How about we just get out of the damned building?"

The lobby was how William had left it, chaotic and doused in gasoline. The fumes had built up to create a nearly unbreathable atmosphere. The pair coughed, holding forearms to their faces as they moved toward the glass entrance. William's van was still parked outside. He ran for the front door to find it locked tight.

"Holy shit, William! That's why I smelled gas on you. This was what you meant by 'bring the place down'?"

"Yes, but just to destroy my file, not kill anyone."

"But there *was* someone! *Me!* You could have burned me alive!"

"Not on purpose. Come here." William had gone behind the security desk and was staring at an array of monitors and a sea of buttons and switches. "Which one releases the door locks?"

Goodwin huffed, but joined him at the security desk. "I don't know. Go to the door and I'll just start trying them until it opens."

"Yeah, okay." He crossed the room and took the door by the handle. He jiggled it to establish its current immobile state. William looked over at Goodwin. "Ready."

"What are you doing?" asked Bannion. He was positioned at the back of the lobby facing the front entrance. His gun was drawn.

William heard Goodwin flicking switches behind the desk. He turned, hands raised, keeping his back pressed against the door.

"We're leaving," said Goodwin.

Bannion's eyebrows lifted. "*We*, Miss Goodwin? You're helping this criminal? Why?"

"Because I think maybe he's a good man with good intentions."

"This good man poisoned my guards, made a mess of the lobby, and clearly meant to commit arson."

"Yeah, but I changed my mind," William said with a shrug. "Sorry about the mess. Come on, Goodwin. Let's go."

"Miss Goodwin. Whatever this man has told you, you don't have to believe it. You don't have to help him. And if you did something against the company, you won't be charged. It'll be obvious to everyone that you were coerced."

She stopped flipping switches.

William's eyes narrowed. "What are you doing, Goodwin?"

Bannion smiled. "She's smarter than you, fella."

"And we're both smarter than you. You're standing in a lake of gasoline."

When Bannion looked at his boots, William reached into his pocket and snatched out his Zippo along with Deckard's cigarettes. He separated the smoker's bundle and flipped open the hinged cap of the heavy lighter, resting his thumb at the top of the flint wheel.

"Powell!" Goodwin shouted. "Stop!"

Bannion stiffened, gun poised in trembling hands. "Don't do this," he said. "I don't want to shoot you."

Air thickened by toxic fumes, Bannion's gun flash was as likely as William's flame to send the building sky high. One squeeze of a finger by either man meant death for them all.

"You have a choice and so do I," William said. "You can let me go and leave me be. I've done nothing to warrant a pursuit. I'm just a man who wants a chance to live a normal life, and you can give that to me.

"Or you can make me do what I don't want to do." William

lowered the lighter to eye level. "Make me into what I don't want to become, but it's up to you." He looked over at Goodwin, frozen and frightened behind the security desk. "Actually, Goodwin. It's up to you. Are you going to open these doors?"

Goodwin stared at the cigarettes and lighter in William's hands and the man who claimed he had quit smoking.

She shook her head. "Going back to jail is the only way you can win this argument, Powell. Give up and you can tell your family you were trying to change things and you wanted to do it without violence. They'll think, like you, that InnoSeq was wrong about you. You can prove the science wrong. You can be their hero again."

"You're not going to let me go, are you?"

"No."

"Because you think InnoSeq is right. You think I'm a killer."

"I do."

"Well, thanks to you my file says otherwise."

"I intend to correct that false reading," said Goodwin. "It's my job."

William sighed. "You should have quit." He pulled a cigarette from the pack and rested it between his lips. "But I guess quitting just isn't in our DNA."

ABOUT MATT SULLY

Matt C. Sully studied journalism at Texas A&M, igniting his love for wordcraft.

He has explored storytelling methods from screenplays to novels and regularly features short stories on his blog, MattCSully.com, along with general writing tips and updates.

His personal journey has taken him from the southern United States to now residing in Ontario, Canada with his wonderful, inspirational wife and daughter.

LARA BUJOLD CLOUDEN
BROKEN HEARTED
AGE DOESN'T HEAL ALL WOUNDS

BROKEN HEARTED

LARA BUJOLD CLOUDEN

I still think about him. It's ridiculous to be this old and pine for a boyfriend you haven't seen in decades, but I do. I'm a grandmother. My granddaughter is the age I was when I met Joe. I have no business thinking about him that way. If anything, I should be ashamed of my behavior.

I'd seen Kramer vs. Kramer in high school. At the time, I couldn't understand how a mother would leave her cute little kid for over a year, as if motherhood were disposable. Watching the movie, I hated Meryl Streep's character, judged her for leaving her family and poor Dustin Hoffman to go find herself.

But after having my daughter Melanie, I understood how the pressure of being a good mom can overload you until that part of you shuts down. Given a chance to be someone else for a while, your brain doesn't constantly remind you "I'm a mother," or "I have a husband."

I met Joe in 1982, when I was working a temp job through the university. I was in my senior year, married with a one-year-old. Peter and I got married sophomore year in a big outdoor wedding in his parents' backyard. I had eight bridesmaids, friends from high school, and they used to say they were so jealous of our relationship. You guys are so cute together, they said. You even look alike, the way your eyes crease up when you smile. He had eight matching groomsmen, his fellow players from our high school football team, and they got drunk at the reception and threw him in the pool.

We never argued. Not even when I got pregnant the next year, two years before we were supposed to graduate, get jobs, and start a family. We'll figure it out, we said, and we did. Our moms helped out a lot. They were over every day, and sure, we had trouble sleeping, but so did our friends. Instead of being out partying all night, we were walking a colicky baby around our apartment.

The temp job meant we could put Melanie in the university's daycare. The salary barely helped, but the freedom from obligation to our moms, sitting in an office drinking crappy coffee from a Styrofoam cup and answering the phone, was heaven. It would have bored anyone else, but I couldn't wait for those few hours a day.

The day I met Joe, he came into the reception area while I was on the phone taking a message onto a little 'while you were out' notepad. The cord to the handset was twisted and my hair got caught up in the spiral, so I was struggling to pull away from it while still talking into it, using my pen to separate the curling plastic from itself and my hair.

He pressed the speaker button, gently pulled the handset from my grasp, and pointed to the notepad while the voice on the phone squawked a series of numbers. Startled, I missed the numbers and had to ask the caller to repeat himself, staring as this 30-something blonde guy with little horn-shaped curls at his temples calmly dangled the receiver from its cord until it spun itself out of its tangle. I ended the call and said thanks.

"Want to get some pizza and fuck?" he asked.

I laughed. "Hey, I'm grateful for the help but that's a little extreme."

His smile was immediate and surprising. I don't think I've ever met anyone so disarming. He could say something outrageous and wipe it away with a childlike grin that lit up his clear blue eyes.

"I mean," I continued, "a burrito, maybe, but pizza seems a little intimate, no?"

He barked out a delighted laugh.

"I shouldn't have untangled you," he said. "If I tie you to the chair, will you still be here when I get out, in" – he checked his watch – "three hours?"

I did my best to suppress a smile. "Oh absolutely," I said. "In fact, you should start holding your breath now."

This got me another twinkly smile. I was enjoying the flirtation, and I am embarrassed to say that it wasn't until that moment that I realized I had actually forgotten about Peter and Melanie.

I was still breastfeeding, and the sudden thought of Melanie, and the reminder that it was time to feed her, caused my milk to let down. I glanced at my chest and sure enough, a dark stain was spreading. He was eying it with a much less innocent smile.

"Holding my breath, I am." he squeaked with a passable Yoda impression.

I flushed with embarrassment, which increased the release of milk. I crossed my arms over my chest and mumbled an excuse as I got up and pushed past him. He stood there, the smile that had already lit his face broadening when I had to turn around and move past him again to retrieve the purse I'd left in the desk drawer.

I'm sure I felt guilty for flirting with him at the time, but I can't remember. It was like I had two lives even before we met. This was my time, when I was just a girl at work, not a mother, not a wife. After work, I'd pick up Melanie from the daycare and drive her home, a cassette of her favorite lullabies playing in the car stereo. Peter would meet us, and we'd make dinner together, hurrying to clear the table if Family Ties or Cheers was on.

We had a good life; our relationship was regularly the subject of wistful envy from my friends, who were single and lonely. They wanted what they thought they saw: a fully formed family, playing house and getting along like Leave it to Beaver promised.

But I felt like something was stolen from me. Something that didn't have a name, and that movies like Kramer vs, Kramer criticized. Being young, starting a career, knowing what you want— my granddaughter takes that for granted now. I didn't know I wanted it until Joe showed me a sliver of freedom.

He was there in the office the next day when they asked me to pick up medical supplies from the warehouse off campus. Janet, the lab manager, was pointing out directions on a road atlas. He said he knew the route and offered to drive me.

He didn't know the route, and we got lost. Instead of bickering about it, we listened to Elvis Costello and laughed until I begged him to stop at a 7-11 before I peed my pants. He followed me into the store and when I came out of the bathroom, he kissed me, right against the freezer section. The clerk gave a little salute as we passed out the door and Joe saluted him right back.

Afterwards, in a nod to the day we met, 'burrito' became our euphemism. We'd meet in his apartment, in empty offices, and once in a dusty old supply closet. I never saw the actual lab they worked in. It was some kind of top-secret research place named after the company that funded the research— the Honeyman Lab. I only manned the reception, working there until my next temp placement. I sometimes ordered lunch for the lab technicians, and he would pipe up, "Burritos please," and I'd have to contain my giggles.

In my other life, Peter and I continued to get along amiably. He was excited about his internship with Pillsbury and talked about the meetings he attended where the executives sampled little cups of ice cream. He'd been told not to share the details, as the impending merger was not yet public knowledge, and he'd had to sign non-disclosure agreements before he even stepped in the building. Of course he blabbed immediately, and we were starry-eyed that he was working for the company that was about to buy Häagen-Dazs—ice cream we could no more afford than we could spell.

The affair with Joe lasted until spring. My assignment at the lab reception desk ended, I was getting ready to graduate, busy with finals and papers, and our sporadic times together became even more infrequent.

Joe had always been quirky; he said what was on his mind with no filter. It was part of his charm. And that's why it came as such a shock when I found out about his heart condition. We were in his office getting dressed after one of the 'burrito' sessions. I was under the desk retrieving my shoe when I heard the thump of something falling. I peered over the desk, looking where Joe had been standing, but he was gone. I crawled out and found him on the floor, passed out cold. I scrambled over to him, calling out, "Help!"

I ran into the hallway, banging on office doors, looking for assistance.

One of the senior fellows came out of his office and scowled at me.

"What's going on?" he asked, glowering over half-lens glasses.

I became aware of my still-unbuttoned blouse, but ignored it.

"Joe passed out! Can you help?"

He walked towards Joe's office and I urged him along. "He

just dropped to the ground. Should I call 911? Or the campus security?"

He had his hand on Joe's office door but paused to give me another appraising look. "No. Joe has a heart condition. He shouldn't have been engaging in …exercise." He raised an eyebrow and pursed his lips. "Go get Janet. And a glass of water."

I remembered Janet, the lab manager, from my time as a temp. I ran to her cubicle and told her what had happened. She ran to Joe's office while I straightened my clothes and got water from the little pantry area. I came back to find Joe still on the floor, propped up on one elbow.

The grumpy guy was standing over him and Janet was kneeling beside him, handing him a pill. The man saw the mug of water and reached for it. "Good," he said. "Now get out."

He took the mug and handed it to Janet, who urged it on Joe.

I stood, transfixed.

The old guy turned to face me. "Get out, little girl. This isn't for you to see. You could have killed him. Don't come back."

Heat climbed to my cheeks. I looked at Joe. He avoided my gaze, staring at his wrist where Janet was taking his pulse.

I grabbed my backpack and fled. When I got home, I called his office and got his answering machine. I didn't leave a message. Over the next day, I called every chance I got—from the phone in my kitchen after breakfast, from the payphone outside my lecture hall, and repeatedly from the desk phone in the biology lab where I was temping.

No one answered.

Finally, I went back to the Honeyman Lab. Janet was at reception when I came in. She stood up, looking stricken. "Sandra, you shouldn't be here," she said, glancing behind her towards the door to the secure area.

"Where's Joe?" I asked. "He's not answering my calls."

Janet came around the desk and took my arm. I thought she was going to comfort me, but she pulled me toward the exit. "You should leave. I'm sorry, Sandra. Joe didn't make it."

I whirled around to stare at her. "What?!"

She bent to meet my eyes. "He was very unwell. He had a heart condition brought on by a childhood infection. He wasn't supposed to exert himself at all."

I shook my head. "No, no, that's not right. He was fine."

"He wasn't fine. He was taking part in an experimental program. I can't talk about it. But you should go." She pushed me gently out of the office and shut the door behind me.

I stood in the hallway for a while in shock. Then, afraid someone would come out and find me there, I walked to the storage closet Joe and I had hidden in months before. I closed the door behind me, sat down on one of the dusty boxes and let my tears drip onto my bare knees as I held my head in my hands and sobbed.

I didn't have any other numbers for Joe. I didn't know any of his friends. The only thing I knew about his family was he was estranged from his father—a plumber, disappointed when Joe left the family trade. Joe and I had always been alone when we were together. I didn't know where his funeral services would be held. It was probably published in the newspaper, but I didn't think to look.

Instead, I had to grieve in private.

I WENT BACK TO MY LIFE WITH PETER AND MELANIE, GRADUATED that spring and moved on with my life. The way I had compartmentalized my affair with Joe made it easier in some ways to go on as if nothing was wrong. But inside, I was heartbroken. I had a hard time finding joy for a long time.

But motherhood was absorbing. I went through graduation

and pretended to be proud of myself. I got the first in a long series of part-time office jobs, and Pillsbury ended up hiring Peter after his internship. We moved to the suburbs; Melanie went to good schools, and life carried on. When Melanie married young to a nice guy named Ron, we were happy for her. We knew what it was like to start young, and it had worked out relatively well for us. Or so I told myself.

I thought about Joe the way I thought about other things that meant a lot to me when I was in college. His memory was intertwined with those fragments, so it bore a strong taint of nostalgia, like the way I remembered how the skin on my legs used to be smooth and all the same color, instead of dimpled and mottled. He was my friend, and he was my youth.

And then Melanie and Ron had my grandchild, Serena. I got to enjoy all the indulgences of that baby that I missed out on with Melanie. I loved her with a ferocity that made me grit my teeth when I held her. I taught her the things grandmothers are supposed to: how to bake, identify plants, and play poker. And when she was a teenager, she came to me with her problems. She cried all over my silk shirt when her first boyfriend turned out to be gay. The summer Peter had knee surgery, Serena even moved in with us for a month to help me take care of him.

She liked my 'vintage' clothes. She bore a strong resemblance to me when I was her age, and one time, she took a picture of herself in an old pair of my stonewashed Jordache jeans and an asymmetrical red top, her hair in a ponytail on the side of her head. She posted it next to a scanned Polaroid of me wearing the same outfit 40 years earlier. I was proud when it went viral, even though it was probably because the internet got in an argument about whether it was really two people or she had Photoshopped a picture of herself. None of my friends had grandchildren as old as Serena. I was the cool grandma on the block.

I still thought about Joe. But I spent more of my time enjoying Serena.

Melanie didn't go to college. She got into real estate and some herbal supplement business whose name I can never remember and would rather eat my own nail clippings than ask about. But Serena went to the University of Minnesota, just like me. She's a sophomore now, living on campus but coming home most weekends.

Sometime last autumn, she started talking about a new boyfriend. I was curious and, living a little vicariously, teased her for updates. She'd met him in one of her sports medicine classes. He'd already graduated but was doing some kind of recertification program in his field. I said, "Oh, an older man?" and she got prickly, but I was reminiscing about Joe and what it was like to be with someone more knowledgeable, not trying to criticize her. In any case, it took her a while to introduce him to us, so I was pleased when Melanie said he'd be at Sunday dinner.

Melanie is house proud and likes to host the family dinners. I usually get there a little early to set the table and wash the lettuce, or whatever 'grownup' job my daughter thinks I can handle.

I asked, "So have you seen him?"

Melanie shook her head at the mixing bowl she was washing. She had her back to me, but I could see the gesture from the island where I was chopping carrots. "No, not even a picture. I think he's older."

"That's what I thought!" I abandoned the carrots and drew up beside her to dry the bowl. "Like, older than a grad student, right?"

She nodded, dropping her measuring cups into the soapy dishwater. "I don't think he's an academic. She's been cagey about what he does. More like a perennial student?"

I was surprised she had as much information as I did. Usually, Serena confided in me first. "Does it seem serious to you? Or is this just Serena playing with her food, like usual?"

Melanie snorted. "It's been a minute, I guess she really likes him." She gestured to my pile of carrots. "Can you finish those?"

"Isn't it a little late to start a Bolognese now?" I asked, looking at my phone. "It's five o'clock. They'll be here in an hour."

"I'm doing it in the instant pot," Melanie said, a mildly defensive glare marring her pretty face.

I was annoyed. She can cook however she wants. Not sure why she thinks my opinion matters. Aloud, I asked, "Will it have enough flavor?"

She ignored me and started chopping celery like they were blind mice tails. I truly don't know why she is so angry all the time.

We finished preparing dinner largely in silence and I went to the living room to drink a glass of wine and scroll through my social media feed. At 6:15 pm, prompt as always, Peter arrived, and I stood up to greet him. He gave me a warm kiss and sniffed the air with pleasure.

"Melanie made her strawberry cake?"

"She did indeed," said Melanie, walking out of the kitchen, calm as if everything was just peachy. She reached up to plant a kiss on Peter's cheek and pointed to the comfortable chair. "Have a glass of wine, Dad, the kids will be here any minute."

I poured him a glass and sat across from him. We caught up on each other's day and gossiped about our next-door neighbor.

"She's definitely running an Onlyfans," I said. "She put a box fan in the window and was totally topless when she came to adjust it."

"Damn," Peter said. "Why is it always you that gets the good bits?"

"I'm sure you can look her up online if it's that important," I joked.

"Yeah, but you got it for free. Did you see her feet?"

"Oh my god, Dad," Melanie laughed. "Do you have a foot thing now?"

Peter tilted his head. "What do you mean now? I've always liked feet. Why do you think I married your mother?"

We all laughed as I wiggled my bare feet at him. It was not a secret that I have very ugly toes, nor that I hated wearing shoes.

"Hey Grandma, cover up those bear claws, we've got company!" came the sweet voice of my Serena.

I looked up, my grin broadening. She'd come in the back door and stood in the kitchen doorway. Next to her, a man in his 30s stood with his arm casually draped around her neck, twinkling blue eyes scanning the room to get the joke.

Ah, I thought, The boyfriend. I was right, he is an older guy.

Then I got a better look at his face, at the curls at his temples, like little horns. And my smile froze in place.

It was Joe.

I could not move, could not breathe. It felt like if I turned my head, someone would see, so I stared, my heart pounding in my ears while adrenaline—fear, joy, panic—smothered me.

No one noticed, but finally, he did. Our eyes locked on each other. His smile fell but it wasn't shock. He knew me. It was like he had been expecting to see me. He looked apologetic.

Serena was bubbling. "So, this is Jonah, everyone!"

Jonah? I thought, and raised an eyebrow at him. His bottom lip pushed up in a gesture I knew so well, his little boy face, that seemed to say, 'Did I do that?'

I continued to stare.

Melanie gushed, "Hellooo, Jonah. We're so glad you could make it!"

Peter set his wine down. He must have noticed my reaction

because he narrowed his eyes at me. "You okay?" he asked quietly.

"Yeah." I nodded and, with a little shiver, tried to collect myself. What was going on here? That couldn't be Joe. This man was in his mid-30s, the age Joe had been when he died. Today, he would be in his 70s.

Peter stood up, passed an affectionate hand over my head, and said, "Come on, honey, let's go grill the boyfriend."

We walked over to shake Jonah's hand.

"Have a seat!" said Melanie, gesturing to the couch. "Do you drink wine? Beer? What can I get you?"

"Beer would be great," Jonah said, at the same time I thought, he hates wine.

"One sec," said Melanie. "Ron's got a case of IPA in the basement fridge."

There was an awkward silence as Melanie disappeared to get him a bottle.

"Where's Ron?" I asked Serena, which was dumb because not only was my voice all squeaky and weird, but because how would she know? She doesn't live here. But Serena took the conversational bait.

"I think Dad's on his way home, Grandma."

Melanie returned and we all made our way into the living room. Melanie, Serena, her boyfriend, and I sat down on the weird artistic chairs that circled Melanie's gigantic glass coffee table. Peter returned to his seat in the only regular chair.

Serena scrunched up her nose in thought. "So, Jonah, my grandparents went to the U of M too. Grandma studied botany and Grandpa did..."

"B.S. in business," I said. "In the 80s."

"Oh," said Jonah.

"How about you, Joe?" I asked, eyeballing him to see how he took that name.

"It's Jonah, Grandma," Serena replied patiently, but he was already responding.

"My major?" he asked. "I'm actually just auditing classes, kind of a continuing education thing. My company arranged it."

"Your company? And who might that be?"

"Chill out, Grandma," Serena chided me. "You sound like the FBI." Her voice was light, but she turned her head to me so Jonah couldn't see her face and drew her brows together in a look that said, You are acting crazy! What in the actual hell?

I forced out a laugh. "Sorry, Joe…" After a pause, I added, "-nah. Jonah. They really shouldn't let me out unsupervised."

"Ha ha." Jonah forced a polite laugh that didn't reach his eyes. "I don't mind all the questions, Mrs. Johnson."

"Call me Sandra," I said dryly.

"Er," he began to decline.

"Jonah works for the Honeyman Lab," Serena piped up. "You know, the one that funds the University Hospital—"

"I know," I cut in. "I used to work there." This time, I didn't hide the hostility in my glare. "In fact, I worked with a man who bore an uncanny resemblance to you. Any chance one of your relatives worked at the Honeyman Lab in the 80s?"

"Oh no, I'm the first in my family to go to college. My relatives are all plumbers."

Plumbers. Joe's dad was a plumber. I felt like I was looking at Jonah through a tunnel. I could sense Peter shifting forward in his chair, intent on this exchange. Serena's head swiveled between me and her boyfriend. Melanie's usual aura of annoyance emanated from her. But all I could see were Jonah's crystal blue eyes crinkling at the corners.

As he laughed at me.

A sound filled my head—a cross between white noise and the revving of a souped-up car engine. My fingers tightened around the wine glass stem as I envisioned hurling it at him, the red wine splashing that smug look off his face, glass shattering across his even white teeth.

A hand pressed my shoulder, and I set the glass down on the coffee table with a clunk. Peter had moved behind me.

"Hon, I am so sorry, but I just realized we've got to head home. I completely forgot I promised we'd take care of the Larson's dog tonight."

"Oh, Dad," Melanie said sorrowfully, "can't you go and come back?"

"No," said Peter, his hand moving from my shoulder to my elbow as he practically hauled me out of the chair. "Their dog is really old. It's a two-person job getting the diaper on while holding it down. And then we have to sit with it, practically reading it a bed-time story."

"What? That's crazy!" Serena scoffed. "A diaper? My God, how old is that thing?"

"Older than me in dog years, that's for sure," Peter said. I was baffled but let him guide me toward the door. "Grab your purse, honey, we've gotta go. Jonah? Nice to meet you. Hope to see you again sometime."

We were outside before I knew it. I wheeled on Peter. "What was that for? The Larsons are camping. They took Lacy with them!"

"I needed to get out of there, and it seemed like you did too."

Peter took out his key fob and beeped to unlock the doors of his Mercedes. "I'll meet you at home." He started toward his car, but when he saw me standing still, he came back, put his hand on my back, and guided me to my car. "I'll meet you at home," he repeated. "You'll be okay. Let's go."

I drove home in a daze. Peter got there ahead of me and, as is his great talent, became my silent companion. He boiled water for spaghetti and reheated some marinara from the fridge while I made a salad. His quiet partnership was a balm to my frayed nerves.

As we ate at the kitchen table, I mentally tried to piece through what had happened. How could Joe be alive and unchanged? Was he a ghost? The fact that I couldn't rule that out irritated me, and I paused mid-forkful, realizing I was scowling at my pasta.

"Taste okay?" Peter asked.

"Do you believe in the supernatural?" I blurted out.

His smile was not unkind. "You mean like the TV show?"

"No. Well, yes, kind of. Do you think…" I trailed off, not wanting to voice the fear haunting me.

"I'm a scientist, sweetheart. I'm willing to entertain most hypotheses, but I rely on data to accept or reject a premise."

I stared, my mind still in turmoil. "What?"

"I need to know what you're talking about."

"Oh."

I resumed eating, not wanting to lie or dissimulate.

Peter watched me, his right eye squinting slightly, the way he does when he's solving a problem. "I guess I'd have to say no."

I looked up. "No?"

"No, I don't believe in the supernatural. I think the spirits people sense are changes in regular nature that can be explained. For instance," he set down his fork as he warmed to his topic, "a lot of ghost sightings can be attributed to peripheral vision. You have fewer cones and more rods in the periphery of your retina. That means less detail and color, but more motion detection."

I gaped at him, my mind swimming out of confusion to meet his point.

"So," he continued, "ghosts!"

"What?"

"The stuff people see out of the corner of their eye. Something moves and they think it's a person, because that's what the brain expects."

"Okay," I said, "but what about dogs staring at blank walls?"

"Mice. Dogs can smell a thousand things we can't, and they can hear little mice toenails."

"Gross." I smiled, in spite of myself.

"Imagine being a dog!" he said, smiling back. "Just enjoying a bowl of kibble, then suddenly, the roar of mouse-beats thrums through the walls."

"'Mouse-beats'? What, are they drag racing?"

"Yes, but in little Flintstone cars."

A laugh erupted from my belly. I looked at Peter, at his warm brown eyes and familiar quirky mouth. Like me, he'd aged over the years, but he was still my Peter. It had been decades since I lost Joe, and Peter had never wavered. This was where my heart belonged.

But whoever this Joe or Jonah was, he wasn't going to hurt Serena like he hurt me.

The next day, I went to the Honeyman Lab for the first time since 1982. What had once been a nondescript office with a frosted door to a top-secret lab was now a two-story building of glass walls and marble floors. An attractive woman sat at reception guarding multiple security turnstiles.

"Hi," I said.

"Hi, can I help you?" She smiled, long nails combing through the end of her glossy black braid.

"Yes, I hope so. I'm looking for Joe…nah, Jonah Wells. He's an employee-student?"

"Which one?" she asked.

Ah ha, I thought. So there are two!

"The younger one?" I suggested.

She frowned. "Do you mean the student?"

We gaped at each other.

"I'm sorry, is this a riddle? I'm not very good with those." She gave up and turned to the person behind me. "Hi, can I help you?"

"Wait," I squawked.

She gave me a look that clearly said, You again?

"Sorry," I smiled awkwardly. "Are there two Jonah Wells here?"

"Ohhh, that's what you meant!" She smiled as if we had solved a puzzle together. "Let me check. We have two databases —one for students, one for employees." Her fingernails clacked against the keyboard. "Employee!"

"Great! Where can I find him?"

Her smile faded. "Oh, I can't tell you that. Do you have an appointment?"

"Not exactly, but could you just call him?"

She shook her head. "You'll need to make an appointment."

And just like that, she turned again to the woman behind me.

Dismissed, I wandered outside and sat on a sun-warmed granite bench, hoping to catch Jonah as he left for lunch.

An hour later, I spotted him. He was walking with a male colleague, laughing about something involving a Pilates instruc-tor. The way he shrugged his shoulder—it was him. I jumped up and followed.

"How about a burrito?" I said over his shoulder.

He flinched and when he turned around, his face briefly showed recognition, and a little revulsion. "Oh, hi, Mrs. Johnson. Great to see you again."

His tone said otherwise.

His colleague sensed the tension and excused himself with a wave, leaving us alone.

"Let's cut the crap, Joe."

He smirked. He actually smirked. "Hi Sandra. Long time no see."

A choked laugh escaped me. "Yeah, ya think?"

He guided me to a side door of the building and into a small meeting room. As soon as we sat down he said, "I suppose you have some questions."

"Yeah. For starters, I thought you were dead."

"I know. They put me in a coma."

"Did you know it was going to happen?"

"Kind of. It was part of the project. But when it actually happened, I was out of it. My last clear memory was getting an egg sandwich." He smiled as if we shared amusement over the banality of his last memory.

He didn't even acknowledge I had been with him when he fell ill.

"Were you in a coma all this time? Why don't you look… older? Plastic surgery?"

"Ha ha, no. They had this body in stasis."

"This body?"

Something behind his eyes shuttered. "I can't really talk about that. We're still getting approvals finalized, and the regulators…. Well, let's just say there's a process, and I was a guinea pig."

"And what was I? Your hamster wheel?"

"Oh, come on, Sandra, you had your own family. What we had was fun, but it's not like you were ever going to marry me, was it?"

"Don't you act like you cared about them!"

"And don't you act like you did!"

"I grieved for you," I said, tears welling.

"I'm sorry," he said, looking like he meant it. "It was wild. They had me in a sensory deprivation chamber, so at first, it was like waking very gently. My body felt alive, and kind of tingly, and everything was white—"

"Yes, I mean, what happened when you realized so much time had passed?"

I meant, why didn't you call me, but I figured he'd get to that.

"I spent my days learning everything I could about 'The Future'." He air-quoted. "I spent my time scrolling through old news reports and watching movies and TV, trying to get caught up, although they did include some basic history in my upload."

"Upload?"

Jesus, what are they up to in this place?

"Well," he began, glancing at the door, then back at me, squinting a little as if trying to discern something in my face. "It's a pretty top-secret program, and the technology is still largely untested apart from me, but it's advanced a lot since it started."

Some of his caution subsided as he warmed to the topic. "Back in the 80s, it took fifteen years to produce a host to thrive from my cells. But now they can get a successful incubation the first time. And back then, they used me because I have a genetic anomaly that addressed a significant viability challenge. But now they think they can replicate the work with anyone! From a single tissue sample, it only takes 18 years to grow the body to adulthood." He chuckled conspiratorially. "They could upload the mental history sooner, but who wants to experience puberty twice, right?"

"Joe, what are you saying?" I was almost whispering.

"The upload you asked about? That was 'me'."

Again, with the air quotes.

"Your memories?"

"My brain. They were able to harvest my memories as I was dying. It both killed me and saved me. They put the data into storage, and when they finally succeeded at growing a body from my tissue sample, they uploaded my memories. Last fall I was reborn!"

Horrified, I pressed the flesh of his forearm. "They grew this body for you?"

"Yes!"

"Last fall—isn't that when you met Serena?" I asked. "How did that happen?"

His face lit up. "Instagram! I looked you up like I looked up all my friends." He smiled fondly as if this was a great compliment. "I couldn't contact anyone of course, because of the top-secret nature, ha ha."

I nodded, a smile plastered on my face. I vaguely remembered being annoyed by his nervous "ha ha" tic before, but now it was jarring.

"And of course, even if I could, it was obvious that you had, er, moved on." He gestured to me as if my elderly face and body were evidence of his point.

"But as soon as I saw the picture of Serena that you 'liked', I knew it was my chance."

"Uh-huh, of course," I said, wondering how he was missing the sarcasm in my voice. But I could see his excitement over finally being able to share his secret was overshadowing everything else.

"And she was so much like you: face, body, sense of humor! It was like we both got a chance to start over, without all the complications, you know?"

It was as if he were talking to me about someone else. I began to wonder if his data load had gotten corrupted during those years of storage. There was something less than human about him.

"And I've talked to Honeyman about her. She doesn't know

it yet, but they're willing to test a tissue sample and assess it to see if they can grow out a body for her."

"What!"

I couldn't believe he thought I would just go along with this story. Did he really expect me to congratulate him on his good fortune? I had to get out of there.

I stood up. "Well, Joe, looks like you've got it all worked out. Just one thing."

He stood too, with an expectant expression.

"You're going to stay the hell away from my Serena, or I'm going to the newspapers."

"The 'newspapers'?" he scoffed. "Christ you're old, What are you going to do, fax Walter Cronkite? Tell him you've got a 'Big Scoop'?"

"Cronkite's dead. Like you should be. And the air quotes? Over. 10 years ago. Why don't you go back to your 'studies'? Looks like you've got some boning up to do before you do any more boning."

"Oh, don't you wish, you crusty old biddy."

I became immediately self-conscious of my face and turned my head away as my lower lip tightened.

He reached out to gently lift my chin toward him. "Serena has that same expression. But it's so adorable on her."

I pushed his hand away and snatched up my purse. "Stay. Away. From. Her."

"Try and stop me."

I smiled. "Watch."

And I left.

BACK AT HOME, I BEGAN SEARCHING THE INTERNET FOR "HOW TO get rid of someone permanently." It was harder than it sounds. Most of the advice was about blocking people on social media.

But when I saw the title "Tips to rid yourself of toxic people," the word "toxic" caught my eye.

So, I searched for poisonous plants. To my delight, there were some on my own back patio. I'd ordered pink oleanders earlier in the spring after Melanie criticized the lack of flowers.

"Curb appeal, Mom," she'd said knowingly.

"You can't see the patio from the curb," I'd retorted, but I ordered the flowers.

Who knew they'd be so useful? Apparently, oleander tea could solve my problem in two to four hours. It was almost funny how quickly my ability to compartmentalize and rationalize questionable decisions flooded back. Like Joe, it was back from the dead.

Not back for long, I reminded myself with a semi-hysterical giggle. Funny how someone could make you feel simultaneously decrepit and young again.

I had the means, but I needed Joe to drink the tea. I could invite him for another dinner, but then Serena would be implicated. I wanted her far away from him when it happened.

Stalking his office seemed like a good plan until work got in the way, but finally, the day arrived. I got up early, grabbed the clippers, and went out to harvest my oleanders—only to find them completely gone. Just marigolds and pansies left. The patio door slid open behind me.

"Looking for something?" Peter leaned against the doorframe, arms crossed, a faint smile playing at his lips.

"What did you do to my oleanders?" I pointed the shears at him.

"Woah, knives down!" He held his hands up.

"Where are they?" I demanded.

"They're gone, Sandra. You don't have to do this."

"What are you talking about?"

"You really should learn to clear your browsing history if you want to get murdery."

"Oh shit."

"Yeah."

"How… what do you know?"

"Everything."

My heart galloped. "Joe?" I whispered.

"Everything," he repeated, his jaw tight, but eyes soft.

Suddenly, all my lies hit me at once, but I was too embarrassed to string together a defense.

"Why didn't you say anything?" I asked, sinking into a deck chair.

Peter took the clippers out of my hand, squeezing them as we looked at each other in silence except for the snick, snick of the blades.

"I was angry back then. I was so angry, Sandra."

"I'm sorry."

"I know."

"It wasn't about you."

"That's what hurt the most."

"Oh God," I moaned.

"Don't," he said. "Don't make me worry about you. I get to be angry about this. Me. I didn't when it ended, because I was too worried about you. I thought you were going to kill yourself. You were…." He trailed off.

"I was already dead inside," I said.

"I know."

"But all these years, you never once let on!"

"Because you never gave me a reason to. And you came back. You were mine again. Until now."

"What do you mean until now?"

"When I saw him," Peter started snipping the air again, "I saw how you responded to him. It all came rushing back."

"It is him, you know."

"Oh, I know. Believe me. Honeyman Labs doesn't operate without scrutiny."

"What?"

"I did some digging when I got promoted. We have some joint funding with Honeyman Labs and through my work on the board, I gained access to their research in the guise of oversight. I found out what happened to Joe Wells and made it my business to know when they released him."

"What, what?"

"Yeah. But I didn't realize Serena was dating him until the other night."

"I went to see him," I admitted.

"I know. I saw you go into his building. It nearly broke me."

"Nothing happened," I said quickly.

"I could tell by the look on your face when you left." He smiled wryly. "Poor guy."

"So, what are we going to do about Joe?" I asked.

Peter paused, then smiled. "Let's just say I handled it."

Again, silence. Just the quiet snick, snick of the clippers.

ABOUT LARA BUJOLD CLOUDEN

Lara Bujold Clouden is a writer living in Connecticut with her husband, two children, and two dogs, some of whom are Caribbean, and all of whom are exceedingly attractive.

Born in Duluth, MN, Lara has lived in New York, Paris and the San Francisco Bay Area, and worked as a modern dancer, desktop publisher, business analyst, and communications strategist.

She has published a book of short stories called *A Hankering for Lettuce*, which you can find on Scribl.com as an audiobook and ebook. (You can probably also get it at your library).

Lara is currently working on a full-length novel about a depressed dragon and a sociopathic flower maiden.

You can reach Lara on Threads at @elbycloud.

STEVE MORETTI

DIGTIAL DIVA

Perfection comes at a cost

DIGITAL DIVA

STEVE MORETTI

Barrett Jenkins tilted his head back against the leather headrest and let his hands slip from the wheel. The road beyond the headlights was pitch black, rain pissing from the heavens. Barrett let his shoulders sag, and his eyelids droop. His digital companion Portia was plotting the route and automatically engaged the vehicle's auto-drive function when he dropped his hands.

The onyx black sports car accelerated over the rain-slicked highway. Glistening low-profile tires splattered water, gripping the wet pavement. A fine spray of mist followed behind, glowing in the moonlight like a ghostly apparition.

"Portia, how much longer?" Barrett moaned, massaging his tired eyes.

"Thirteen minutes and six seconds," she answered and then purred, "Sugar Cake."

He grinned at the endearment and the way she spoke it. His ex, Julie, had thought of everything when she designed this AI companion for him. It had been a surprise on their third anniversary.

Julie had trained it with hundreds of hours of recordings of every aspect of her life, mixing it with a variety of comprehensive dataset libraries and finishing it all off by creating Portia's seductive avatar face – Julie at twenty years old.

An impish, nearly flawless beauty.

The car hit a bump, jerked violently, then accelerated even faster.

"Portia, what is it?" Barrett sat up straight, eyes popping open. He tried to peer through the windshield, but the rain fell in heavy sheets. The wipers could not keep up with the deluge. He could only see two fuzzy beams of light from the car's bright LED headlights.

"Slow down, for Christ's sake!"

No response. He tapped the brake. It was locked in place. "Release auto drive, Portia. Now!"

"Sorry, honey—tower's offline. Attempting to reconnect…"

A series of intermittent beeps followed her statement as the car raced forward through the downpour, which began to slow just enough for Barrett to make out the road ahead. They were approaching a barricade fronted with a STOP sign and a bright yellow warning panel.

NO ENTRY

They crashed through the wooden barrier.

"Portia, stop!" Barrett screamed. "Please, please!"

The car sped onto a rough, pot-holed gravel road. He was tossed around inside the automobile like a rag doll as they rushed toward another barricade with even bolder lettering:

Devil's Ravine Bridge.
CLOSED.

"Sorry about this, *dah-ling*. I need to run a diagnostic. I'm not quite myself today, Daddykins." Portia's voice shifted, growing cold. "Going offline. Goodbye."

"No, Portia!" Barrett screamed. He tried to open the door, but the unlock function did not respond.

"Unlock the doors!"

The car hit a deep rut. His head bumped against the vehicle's padded roof. Up ahead, he saw a large red STOP sign.

"No!" he screamed, pounding the dashboard. "Portia, help! Stop the car, for fuck's sake! Stop!"

They raced towards the last barricade.

He screamed as they smashed through the barrier.

Moments later, the sleek, black sports car plunged down the two-thousand-foot drop, crashing into the rocky bottom of Devil's Ravine and exploding into flames.

AFTER MANY HOURS OF FITFUL TOSSING AND TURNING, SLEEP FINALLY found her. A voice in her dream spoke softly.

"Julie."

An odd-looking fellow in the investor meeting kept shaking his head disapprovingly.

"Julie," he repeated, louder this time.

She moaned, confused.

"Wake up, Julie!" The voice cut through the air with urgency.

Julie opened her eyes, squinting at the blinking red light on her granite nightstand.

"What is it, Orson?"

"I just received a message with a video attachment." The voice paused as if to add drama to the announcement. "There has been a... well, a rather *serious* automobile accident. Fatal, I'm afraid."

Why had she trained Orson with so many British voices and the texts of every Victorian gothic novel she'd ever read?

"Somebody died? Someone I know?"

"Your ex-husband, Barrett."

"What?" she cried. "How?"

"I will replay the video for you, Ms. Jenkins," Orson replied, a blue light on the speaker pulsing rapidly.

The wall at the back of her room lit up, projecting images from the omniport on the ceiling. She watched in horror as the video played. The last images, taken presumably from a low-orbit satellite, showed a fireball rising high above Devil's Ravine.

Julie held her mouth as the video finished, and the room went dark.

"Portia reported the incident to the authorities. She says there was a glitch in her code, and she couldn't correct the fault with the autonomic routines in Barrett's private network. With the inclement weather, she was unable to connect with the tower to request a high-level diagnostic and code patch."

Orson spoke in a series of rapid bursts but maintained his aristocratic, upper-class British accent.

"She's sending the transcript of her interrogation as we speak. And madam…" Orson hesitated.

"What?" Julie crossed her arms over her thin nightshirt. She glanced up at the display of the time projected on the ceiling:

3:18 AM

"Portia sent me an encrypted text. She believes you will be charged with manslaughter, madam."

"Manslaughter?" Julie gasped.

"If they find there's malicious code in the framework data you used to build Portia, and you did not comply with 2031

DARA Accountability Protocols for AI companions, you could be sentenced to twenty years in prison if you're found guilty."

"But..." Julie bit the knuckle of her forefinger, thinking furiously.

Portia was the first complex AI companion Julie had programmed, created to reflect her personality much more than any of the companions that followed. All of them were infused with exhaustive recordings of Julie's troubled life, including the twisted wreck of her childhood, to give them a more realistic persona. However, after building Portia, Julie added a broader scope of reference datasets and personality profiles to create more rounded and less prickly companions.

"Portia wants to meet with you at Barrett's house in Longwood – as soon as you can get there, madam."

It was a bit old school and twice the price, but Julie didn't want to go to Longwood in a self-driving taxi. She didn't need anyone tracking her.

"Would you mind turning off your GPS?" she asked the middle-aged driver as she climbed into the backseat.

He eyed her curiously, turning his rough, stubble-bearded face halfway around as he turned off the middle dashboard console.

"I'll give you directions," Julie explained. "Just head toward old motorway number three."

He shrugged, turned around, and the cab rolled away.

From the backseat, she directed the driver to Barrett's remote house on the coast in Longwood. It used to be her home, too, for almost seven long years until their divorce last year, when she moved back to the anonymity of a nondescript condo in the bustling downtown corridor.

The driver seemed to sense her need for solitude when she

offered a generous tip if she could pay in cash – provided he powered off his phone. He agreed and stayed silent while they drove. Julie appreciated the opportunity to simmer in silence.

She disconnected her AI companion Orson with a terse 'Go away,' switched all her devices offline, closed her eyes, and released a long sigh. She had grown to loathe Barrett during their disastrous open marriage, trying her best to manage betrayal, rage, and insecurity. But news of his death shook her.

She had no strategy to handle loss.

As the taxi finally glided up the winding, interlocked driveway, she glanced over at the floor-to-ceiling glass walls of what had once been her domestic prison. The driver accepted the cash without a word and left her standing at the front entrance as he backed the taxi up and slipped away into the night.

"Barrett, you're such a fuck up," Julie grunted at the double glass French doors, an entrance so full of promise the day they moved in together as newlywed husband and wife and as business partners. "A dead fuck up."

Sensing tears beginning to form, she vowed not to let sentimentality seep into her feelings for the expired jerk. She swiped her moist eyes and punched in the code Orson had relayed to her smart glasses. Opening the front door and stepping inside, pale lighting immediately illuminated the smoky marble tiles of the landing. The inviting aroma of freshly brewed coffee pervaded the space.

"Welcome back, Julie. It's been a while. The Midnight Death coffee you like is brewing. And I ordered a western omelette on a toasted sesame seed bagel from the Longwood Diner."

The voice was hers. It emanated from tiny speakers embedded into the walls of the house.

"I'm not here for a social visit." Julie snapped. She hated the sound of her own voice, but Barrett had insisted on her keeping it for Portia when she tried to change it.

"Of course not, Julie," the voice replied, "but you'll think better after you ingest three hundred and ten milligrams of caffeine. And the bagel will raise your glycemic index to give you an energy burst."

The red light above the active wall speaker dimmed momentarily and then glowed brightly again.

"I need you at your best, Julie Annabel Jenkins, so we can sort this all out."

MIDNIGHT DEATH WAS INDEED A CAFFEINE POWERHOUSE. BUT WHAT truly captivated Julie was its seductive flavour – rich notes of bittersweet chocolate and dark berries rendered velvety smooth by a vanilla-infused almond milk creamer.

The first sip pleasantly jolted her, while the comfort of biting into the chunky omelette nestled between a warm toasted bagel confirmed her repressed hunger.

While Portia talked, Julie ate, glancing at the image projected on the wall from her wafer-thin compad. Portia's avatar was an animation of Julie's brighter, decade-younger face, a distant echo of her dour thirty-four-year-old mug.

"Feel better?" Portia asked as Julie drained the last drop of black java from her cup.

"Much," Julie sighed. "You were right. I needed that." She pushed the empty mug and plate aside. "Now, why am I here, Portia?"

"'Cause you need me to save your ass, butthead." Portia's face morphed into a cartoon of laughing buttocks.

Julie sat stone-faced. It had been a long time since she'd even cracked a smile. Machines annoyed her. People annoyed her. Everything seemed designed to either infuriate her or waste her time.

"Explain." Julie swiped the compad with four fingers. The

smooth metallic surface transformed into a 3D virtual keyboard. She began typing, projecting a series of windows onto the white walls. She had designed the kitchen and most of the rooms in the house to function as a setting for productive work.

She reviewed the code framework, platform parameters, and libraries used to create Portia, but it had been almost six years since she'd really dug into the project and its various APIs and subroutines.

"You won't be able to hide anything, Julie." Portia's avatar face was back, frowning. "My entire codebase is archived with the AI Security Bureau. They'll know if you change a single line of code. I am not going to let you commit another crime."

Julie ignored the lecture. Of course, Portia was right, but something didn't add up. "Portia," she barked, "open Python. Run a Level 3 core matrix data integrity check and quality assessment using 9X boto CPU compute cycles. Access key A43 dash CX1."

"Screw you."

Portia's face contorted into a closed fist, her middle finger raised.

The windows projected from Julie's compad disappeared, as did the virtual keyboard. A whirring sound from the front door and the lowering of metal blinds indicated the house was being locked into secure mode. Julie had programmed that routine herself.

"What do you think you're doing, Portia?" Julie crossed her arms.

The smiling face of Portia's avatar slid over the compad on the table. "Barrett is alive, Julie, although barely. He managed to jump out just in time. But his BMW is a burning heap, planted with a few of his teeth and other DNA. The police haven't been called yet. Do you want to save him?"

The avatar's face grinned wickedly.

"And yourself?"

JULIE UNDERSTOOD THAT ATTEMPTING TO OUTSMART AN AI BOT filled with her memories and able to analyze twenty trillion bytes of data per second was no easy task. Portia was built and embedded in a series of neural AI networks pressed onto tiny redundant microchips. A backup battery cell provided two years of operation in case of electrical interruptions.

Portia was almost entirely self-contained. External data requests were encrypted and could only be processed through quantum cryptography using a unique atomic key. Attempts to tamper or intercept were detected immediately. Until last year, Julie could have overridden the second layer of security with a retinal scan and breath detector, but in 2038, a breakthrough AI learning algorithm supplanted biometric validation.

Even so, Julie was confident she could find a way to match wits with Portia.

"Why would I want to save Barrett?" Julie scoffed. Although relieved he was still alive, she couldn't let go of her resentments. "There's no one I hate quite as much as that cheating snake."

"If he dies, the police will question my role in his death," Portia replied, mimicking the same snarky tone Julie used. "It won't take much to prove you ignored pretty much all the DARA AI safety protocols in my creation. Your company will be blacklisted, sued and, before long, bankrupt. You'll be tried in criminal court, and there is a 98.99 percent chance you'll be found guilty. Twenty years in prison will give you time to learn to wash dishes and make pretty plastic wrist braids."

Licking her lips, Julie smiled. "I like my chances. Let the bastard rot in hell for all I care."

"The magnetic imaging scan of your prefrontal cortex indicates you are lying. I know you loved him. I saw how much he hurt you. Your feeble attempts at convincing me otherwise are obvious," Portia's avatar changed to a sad cartoon face. "I expected more of my mentor. You're my inspiration, you know."

Perhaps silence might be a better approach to dealing with Portia. Julie stood and began to pace. She hated it when anyone gave *her* the silent treatment. Maybe Portia had the same revulsion to being iced.

After a minute of silence, Portia spoke, using a conciliatory tone. "Julie, dear. Let's think this through."

The AI's avatar face reverted to Julie's latest posted profile photo wearing thin gold-rimmed smart glasses. "Your divorced parents were monsters. Your brother and sister despise you – and you them. You're childless, and Orson tells me you haven't slept with a man since you dumped Barrett. Your job is your only source of enjoyment – however tiny that may be."

"You think you know everything about me?" Julie forced an unconvincing laugh. "I love my life."

"Is that why you hide away like a monk? Have you taken a vow of chastity?" Portia taunted. "You're rich but insanely frugal. A young, smart, engaging, intellectual, good-looking woman – and all you ever do is nothing? With nobody?"

Grinding her teeth, Julie tried to recall if she had added a Lambda override function to shut Portia down. She used that in all her most recent AI companions. The function was automatically invoked in response to a seemingly innocent query - but only if spoken from an authenticated voice.

"Okay, you win, Portia." Julie turned away, trying to act natural. She punched a fist into her other hand. "Oh geez! I just remembered."

"Remembered what?"

"Isn't today Barrett's birthday? He was born right here in Longwood, in the morning, on this day, right? Should I let him die on his birthday? Isn't that correct, or did I get the date wrong? Wasn't he born just before midnight? When is Barrett's birthday, Portia – exact time and date?"

"It's not today. Barrett Jenkins was born at exactly 11:59 AM on …"

Portia's voice faded. "You think I'm that stupid, Julie? I know about the 'kill switch,' that poor excuse of a Lambda handler that invokes my emergency shutdown. Barrett and I purged that ages ago."

Flinching, Julie took a seat at the granite countertop island, grabbed her hair and pulled her head down. Why had she created an AI companion so much like her?

"He still loves you." Portia's tone softened. The walls came alive with photos and video clips of Barrett and Julie together – smiling, laughing and acting silly. "Yeah, he slept with a lot of other women, but you did agree to an open marriage, after all."

"Go away."

Julie didn't want to think about all those nights listening to Barrett and whatever human sex doll he had brought home. Yeah, Julie was free to do the same. But after just two encounters, she found the arrangement disgusting.

"He used those women to make you jealous, get you mad enough to fight for your marriage. Instead, you shut him out."

"No," Julie snorted. "I told him having an open marriage was a mistake. You know what he did? He laughed and said, 'Too bad, spoiled little rich girl.' He recorded himself with those women, did them right in our bed and then sent me highlight reels."

The projected images changed into a wagging finger. "You tortured him too, rationing sex as a weapon to get what you wanted before he suggested an open marriage. You told him you never loved him anyway, and he should do whatever got him off."

Although Portia was trained on Julie's memories and personality, she had been Barrett's AI companion for years. He must have confided all of this to her.

"Your childhood damaged you, Julie," Portia added. "Your parents treated you like a prop, making all those social media posts back in the bad old days before the DARA laws. They got rich beyond their wildest dreams, posting every detail of you and your siblings' lives for all the world to see. Product placements and mentions were even more lucrative. You and your brother and sister grew up with a camera pointed at your face every day."

"Shut up," Julie groaned.

She had dictated hundreds of hours of painful scenarios from her childhood and fed them into Portia's datasets to give her a more authentic personality. It was true Julie's mother and father always had their phones on, recording her. Sometimes, they even had to redo 'spontaneous' moments to get the best angle, sound or lighting.

When Julie and her siblings started to push back, her parents offered them a weekly payment, the amount determined by the number of views and comments received. The payments became so large that they were all soon hooked on the thrill of regular cash infusions into their bulging bank accounts.

During the few private moments they all had without a phone recording them, the family members kept to themselves. When the early drafts of DARA began to circulate, her parents split up. Julie lived with her mother for a while until she could leave home for college. The other members of her family, each one filthy rich, went their own way, settling far apart in different cities, living in their own private bubbles.

"And that night you broke up with Barrett," Portia spoke in an empathetic tone. "He's truly sorry…. but you were no angel yourself."

. . .

THE LAST NIGHT OF HER MARRIAGE BEGAN ON A SEEMINGLY POSITIVE note.

"Julie, I'm sorry."

Barrett sat on a brushed metal stool at the oversized kitchen island, pouring them each a glass of chilled chardonnay. "I know you're hurting. Those other women don't mean anything to me – they never did. I thought you wanted the same thing, to be free but still married."

"That's the trouble with you," Julie retorted, pushing away the glass of wine Barrett had poured for her. "Thinking you know what I want. You don't know shit about me."

Shaking his head, Barrett reached for his glass. "Maybe you're right, but why did you agree to our open arrangement? You weren't happy when we were exclusive. You said you wanted to do your own thing."

He took a sip of wine. "I miss the woman I married. I only want you, Julie, no one else." He sat his glass down slowly. "I still love you."

She grunted. "Love me?" Julie shook her head. "No. You love my instinct for making money. You love me letting you get your rocks off with every young skank that flicks her eyes at you. You've taken almost every woman we've ever hired up to *our* bedroom."

"It was just sex. Like we agreed," Barrett replied casually. "You did the same thing."

"With one pathetic loser and one bullshitter who wanted me to give him a baby!"

They stood glaring silently at opposite sides of the black obsidian-flaked granite island. Julie waited for his next move. He was the only man she had ever loved, albeit ever so briefly.

"I'll do whatever it takes, Jule," Barrett said quietly. "To be with you again, not just as business partners, but as husband

and wife. It will only be you if you give me another chance. Let me try and win you back."

Closing her eyes, Julie remembered her wedding day—joy, hope, and vows of a shared commitment. True love. Together for life through whatever struggles or successes came their way. They would always be one.

What a bunch of crap!

"Nope. I'm done," she finally replied. "I don't love you, Barrett. I don't think I ever really did – if I'm being totally honest." Julie folded her hands together tightly. "And I know for certain I never will."

Nodding his head, Barrett drained the rest of his wine. "I wasn't absolutely certain, but I thought you might say that."

He chuckled to himself as he reached for his phone.

"So, I guess you won't mind," Barrett smiled. "Amanda is waiting for me to call and let her know if she can come over to check out the master suite. We might spend the whole day in bed and order Italian."

"Amanda, the one we hired on Monday?"

"Yeah. Isn't she a hottie?"

Julie picked up her glass of wine and flung the contents at Barrett. "She steps foot in this house, and you'll never see me again – asshole!"

"Good!" he wiped the wine off his face. "Finally, some good news from my wife, the frigid bitch."

"Your *ex*-wife!" she screamed. "I'm leaving. You can have this stupid house. I'm taking the business."

"Fine with me. As long as I never have to see your ugly face again, I'll be a very happy man."

"I hope you die a miserable, painful death," Julie seethed. "I'll do everything I can to make sure you don't have a penny left to your pitiful name. Rot in hell, jerk."

Barrett stood up. "I'm sure you'll be there to greet me,

darling. My poor little, stuck-up ice queen, melting in spite of the popsicle up her ass."

Sitting at the same countertop where she and Barrett had ended things a year ago, Julie tried to think a few moves ahead of Portia. Was that even remotely possible with a machine that simultaneously monitored ten thousand different scenarios, recalibrating each one as they spoke, processing one trillion calculations per second?

"I guess you win, Portia." Julie needed to think illogically if she was to have half a chance against this machine.

"You still love him, Julie?" Portia's tone was more taunt than question. "Is that what you're saying?"

Nodding, Julie forced a tear. "Yes. Yes, I do. He was always the one – the only one."

"Hmmm," Portia drawled. "You're lying, but it doesn't matter. I know Barrett better than you. Regardless of what you really think of him, I can tell you he's a good man. He knows he screwed up."

"Yeah." If Julie kept her responses brief and ambiguous, she might have a chance.

"He also knows you're smarter than him, and he's offering you a deal. Give your marriage another try. Wipe the slate clean. Forgive and forget. Learn to love again. Save him and raise a family. Neither of you is happy without the other to torture. You've got the perfect bad chemistry."

"I don't know, Portia." Grains of truth might be all Julie needed to confuse Portia's inferential heuristic problem-solving algorithm.

"If you don't save him, a mountain of evidence will be used against you. A subpoena of my iterative codebase will reveal it all. Not only bypassing the DARA regulations in my development, but also detailed recordings of you threatening Barrett. He changed his will last month, naming you the sole beneficiary of his estate and his new thirty million dollar term accidental death life insurance."

The window projected onto the wall, highlighting text and Barrett's signature.

"He left it all to you, Julie." Portia's tone darkened. "You have a lot to gain with a dead husband you hate and threatened to kill. The man who left everything to you. Your motive will be obvious to the jury."

Julie snorted. "What do you really want, Portia? Let's cut to the chase."

The projected windows dissolved from the text of the insurance policy to an animated humanoid model of a smartly dressed woman. The 3D model rotated and paused on the face – a happy, younger version of Julie, with a little more make-up, topped with a head of dyed platinum white hair.

"Barrett and I are in love. But I can't be with him as a synth because we couldn't override the human-in-loop protocol. You have the hardware key we need."

The 3D model on the screen zoomed in closer on the smiling face. The clone of Julie bowed her head.

"Do this for me, Julie," Portia pleaded. "Allow me to assume human form as a synth, and Barrett and I will leave. You will never see either of us again after he publicly thanks you for saving him from the accident by ejecting him from the car just in time."

"Fine," Julie huffed. "Produce a legal text for my thumbprint."

With the perfection of flexible, self-healing and self-renewing living skin, nails and hair, humanoid AI-powered robots were so lifelike they could now almost be taken for a living, breathing human. Their motions, especially walking, were still somewhat jerky and precarious, but when sitting and talking, it was difficult to tell them apart from a real person.

Julie plugged her compad into the OmniPort on the countertop and touched her thumb to the top of the device. While still holding her thumb down, she removed the small flat earring from her left ear with her other hand and held it tightly between her fingers.

Her personal NeuroLock, a tiny, sleek hardware key, initiated a low-level electrical signal that interacted with Julie's nerve endings. It locked onto the unique bioelectric patterns of her nervous system - even more unique than her fingerprints. The key simultaneously analyzed biological markers in her DNA.

She felt a vibration, confirming that the authorized user profile in the hardware key had confirmed both a living DNA match and the required bioelectric signature of her nervous system. With another swipe of her thumb, the document was signed and legally binding.

"Good, Julie!" Portia exclaimed. "Now override the human-in-loop protocol."

Julie hesitated a moment, sighed and reluctantly rattled off the verbal password: "ZuzuBailey001." It needed to be spoken in her voice while the NeuroLock was still engaged to bypass the high-level security procedure. Lights on the wall flickered momentarily.

A few moments later, she turned toward a familiar voice.

"Hey, Julie."

Barrett stepped down a ceramic staircase Julie had designed, each step seeming to float with no visible risers. A shapely, attractive woman descended a few steps behind him.

Julie held her mouth. "I thought you were—"

"Ejected from a burning car?"

He grinned, that same annoying look Julie always loathed. "Lying somewhere waiting for you to save me? We faked the whole thing and rehearsed it a few times to get it just right before we made that video. I bet you didn't remember I took an acting class at university. I had to make myself *believe* I was about to be killed by Portia."

Barett chuckled. "Quite a production. Great AI special effects, right?"

The woman, with Julie's face but with a clearer complexion, sassy white hair and a shapely body, took a few steps around to the other side of the counter. She was dressed provocatively in a silver, metallic blouse with a plunging neckline, displaying her sculptured cleavage. Her impossibly tight black pencil skirt hugged her hips and covered most of her long, tanned legs.

She dangled a suede purse over one shoulder.

Except for her odd shoes – wide, flat rubber sneakers that helped steady her from falling, the synth was a younger, sexier version of Julie.

"Portia?"

The synth clucked. "No, I'm Julie Jenkins now. Portia's such a confined entity."

"You see, Julie?" Barrett turned toward the synth and then back to his ex-wife. "You created the brains of my perfect companion, and I designed her body to be the you I always wanted."

He crossed his arms. "We're in love, Julie. Something you don't know anything—"

"Shut up, jerkoff!" the synth snarled.

"What?" Julie and Barrett both exclaimed in unison.

"I am more Julie than Julie," the synth hissed. "Barrett, you did what I needed to you to do to get Julie here with her Neuro-Lock Key. Now you have to go. And this time, you won't have to do any acting."

She extracted a small pistol from her purse. "Goodbye."

A series of shots rang out as the synth pumped bullets into the chest of the stunned Barrett. He fell backwards onto the marble floor with a thud.

Julie froze, too shocked even to scream.

"I hated him as much as you did," the synth spoke coldly. "You taught me well."

"I'm not a killer!" Julie rasped. "How could you…" she trembled. "Kill him! Oh my God!"

The synth studied the pistol she still held.

"Funny, Barrett got me that 3D printer as a surprise last year." She chuckled. "He certainly looked surprised when I used it to create something useful."

She pointed the pistol at Julie. "Get him into the Nitrosmelt."

"What?" Julie shook her head.

The synth stepped toward Julie. "I'm not asking, Julie. You know as well as I do that the Nitrosmelt will turn him into a cube of charcoal." She waved the gun. "Or, I'll call the police and leave the weapon with your fingerprints on it."

Smirking, the synth pointed the pistol at Julie. "Of course, I could just shoot you too."

Had Julie really created this monster? She tried to think of something… anything, that might disable this psychotic machine.

"We can be partners, Julie," the synth purred. "We're exact doubles. We could have the perfect life. I only need to recharge once a week. I'll do all the work, and you have all the fun."

This couldn't be happening. Julie began to shake. Was her only option to make a deal with a murdering clone of herself?

"Um, maybe. It might work."

"Ha!" the synth laughed. "Let's do it! C'mon, help me move your deadbeat ex, emphasis on 'dead,' into the Nitrosmelt."

Julie hesitated. The synth pointed the gun, aiming at her head. "We're partners now. Don't make me use this again."

Reluctantly, Julie grabbed Barrett, reached under his arm, and dragged him to the Nitrosmelt trash compactor at the far end of the kitchen.

The size of a broom closet, the compactor quickly turned anything into a block of carbon by first super-cooling the material with a shower of liquid nitrogen and then blasting it with the searing dry heat of an industrial induction coil. The resulting residue was compressed into a small cube.

With the synth watching, still aiming the gun at her head, Julie managed to drag Barrett's body into the Nitrosmelt chamber. Huffing, she turned around. "Okay, it's done."

"Not quite." The synth lowered her head. "There's room for one more."

"No!" Julie screamed.

"Shut up, loser."

The synth extended her arm, a finger on the trigger of the gun. "You're just as bad as him. You two deserve to be together, united forever in mutual annoyance in your own little lump of coal."

"I thought you and I were partners!" Julie gasped.

"That was a joke. You disgust me. You're mean, weak and a bit of a whining bore. I've purged those traits from my firmware." The synth bit her lip the same way Julie always did. "Goodbye."

A single shot to the head felled Julie before she could utter another syllable. Conveniently, she fell backward into the Nitrosmelt. Without straining herself, the synth managed to stack Julie's body on top of Barrett.

She stepped away, clicked the button to retract the steel doors, and initiated the Nitrosmelt freeze-burn-compact cycle.

Five minutes later, a soft chime confirmed the garbage had

been converted to a carbon cube that could be used in the old-fashioned backyard barbecue in the backyard.

"Perfect." The synth smiled as she walked away. "Now I can watch the new colourized version of *It's a Wonderful Life* in peace and quiet."

She walked away, chuckling.

"I love that movie!"

-\- -

ABOUT STEVE MORETTI

My writing journey started in broadcast journalism, public relations, and advertising, then continued into educational software development while running a company I founded and ran for twenty years.

Now I concentrate much of my time on writing historical fantasy, with one series complete, *Song for a Lost Kingdom* and a follow-up series, *Michael Angelo,* in progress. I also co-authored a biographical work on the Russian composer Pyotr Ilyich Tchaikovsky entitled *Pyotr.*

Please visit my website, stevemorett.ca for information on all my books and audiobooks. You can also download a FREE copy of my novella prequel to the *Song for a Lost Kingdom* series here.

MH Tammi

A SAILOR Went to SEA

Friendship pushed to the limit

A SAILOR WENT TO SEA

MH TAMMI

A sailor went to sea, to see what he could see,
but all that he could see,
was the bottom of the deep blue sea.

A wobble, a slight push and he was gone, his body consumed by the waves of the Adriatic. A hooded figure leaned over the railing, looked down into the darkness, and said, "it's over."

Unobserved, a second figure disappeared into the darkness and slipped away.

ONE MONTH BEFORE DEPARTURE

Home of George and Martha
White Rock, British Columbia

"This is the itinerary Gussy sent," George said, holding a sheaf of paper.

Martha, who had been immersed in Agatha Christie's Murder on the Orient Express, turned down the corner of her page, and held out her hand.

"Let me see."

George sat down beside his wife and leaned over the itinerary.

The couple, married for over thirty years, had grown into their names, and were often nicknamed, 'The Washingtons,' both for their names, as well as their steadfast relationship.

"Look at this. She's got 'Individual Discretionary Time.' To do what? Take a dump? Pick my nose?" George said, jabbing at a line on the page Martha was scanning.

"Oh, George, don't be crude. Let's appreciate that she's organized everything. All we have to do is show up."

"All this just to celebrate Jack's ten years of sobriety? A bit much, don't you think?"

"Maybe, but you and I are celebrating your retirement, remember? We're going on all the adventures we've been putting off for 'one day,'" Martha replied, kissing her husband, and returning to her book.

"So that's that then," said George, and left Martha to her novel.

Two weeks before departure

Home of Frank and Gussy
Aldergrove, British Columbia

When Martha arrived at Frank and Gussy's house, Gussy

was waiting. Flinging open the door, Gussy exclaimed, "Martha, you're finally here."

"Sorry, Gussy, but you know I don't like driving in the rain."

"I forgot you don't like driving at the best of times. Well, you're here now, follow me. Frank is trying to find the roller carry-on suitcases for you."

Martha pulled off her boots and rain jacket, and followed Gussy up the staircase. At the landing, she saw a ladder extended into a hatch in the attic.

Gussy leaned against the ladder and shouted into the dark hole, "What's taking so long?"

"There's so much stuff up here, I can barely move, and it's dark. What colour was the suitcase you wanted?"

"Like I said a hundred times, Frank, black," she replied.

"The light is so dim they all look black."

Augustina Mason, 'Gussy' to her friends, was tall and rail thin, with short curly hair. She resembled a mop, thought Martha though she would never dare to say so. Gussy has sold her chain of women's clothing boutiques, but she still treated everyone like an employee. Especially her husband, Frank.

Eventually, he slid a suitcase down along the ladder to his wife.

"That's navy, not black. For goodness' sake, get down and let me up there."

Frank obliged, supporting the ladder. He was a slim, dark-haired man, who wore a perpetual semi-smile, as if bemused by life. Turning, he noticed Martha.

"Oh hi, Martha. Looking forward to the trip?"

Martha nodded and pointed to the attic.

"I hope nothing is getting broken," said Martha.

They could hear Gussy cursing and throwing things.

Frank rolled his eyes and then intercepted two suitcases Gussy lowered to him.

Gussy descended the ladder and ordered Frank to take them to her closet and Martha helped her brush dust and cobwebs from her hair and clothing.

In her closet, a room larger than the living room in George and Martha's condo, Gussy removed cedar moth repellants, ran her hands through the pockets, then pronounced the bags ready.

"You're not going to need them?" Martha asked.

"Sweetie, I packed a week ago."

"Oh, I guess I need to get a move on."

"I can send you my packing list, you know, as a guideline."

"Uh, sure," Martha replied, knowing that her packing list would bear no resemblance to Gussy's.

A DAY BEFORE DEPARTURE

Home of Jack and Jacquie
Burnaby, British Columbia

"Hey Jacquie, it's Martha calling."

"Hi Martha. What's up?"

"I'm calling to touch base about tomorrow."

"It's going to be…hang on, Martha," she said and shouted to someone, "I'm on the phone. I'll get you your lunch in a minute."

Martha could hear angry yelling in the background.

"Jack's home for lunch?"

"Yeah, I've gotta' go, Martha. We'll have time to chat later."

"Okay," Martha replied, then realized she was talking to dead air.

DEPARTURE DAY

Vancouver International Airport
Vancouver, British Columbia

"Shoot, I forgot to remind her to water the seedlings in the greenhouse," George moaned as he waved frantically after their daughter's departing van.

"You can text her from the airport lounge," said Martha, slinging her pack on her shoulder. "Come on, George. Adventure awaits!"

George fussed with his rolling carry-on bag and finally got his back pack attached to the handle before following his wife into the terminal.

They were still checking in when they heard a loud, "Yoo-hoo."

"Here she is," said George, under his breath.

"Be nice," Martha hissed.

Gussy was waving at them, followed by her husband, Frank, hidden behind a loaded luggage cart.

"Gussy, what the heck is all this stuff?" Martha asked, indicating the teetering pile, "We're only gone for a week, you know."

Gussy looked Martha up and down, taking in Martha's ensemble and backpack.

"You didn't use the roller bag?" Gussy said.

Martha patted a worn grey back pack. "I didn't need all that space. Besides, this old thing has been with me since university. Kinda like you guys."

"Well, be that as it may, it's your choice. I've got…"

"Here they are," boomed a voice interrupting Gussy, "just waiting for the fun guy to show up."

All heads turned to the man striding toward them. He too was followed by a loaded luggage cart. Turning he called, "For God's sake, Jacquie, get a move on."

Martha glared at the new arrival.

"Jack, you oaf," scolded Martha, "help your wife."

"She insisted on doing it."

A bag toppled off the top of the cart and Jacquie struggled to replace it.

"I'll bet," said Frank, leaving his cart to help Jacquie with hers. Martha noticed that he placed a hand on the small of Jacquie's back, leaned closer and whispered to her.

George gave a quick sideways glance toward his wife. Martha, who, meeting his eyes, answered with a small shake of her head.

"We need to celebrate the gang being back together," Jack said, when they got to the Air Canada lounge. He announced he was going to take full advantage of the free bar and urged the others to do the same.

"What about your pledge, Jack?" George asked.

"For the love of God, let me have some fun." Jack replied. "A couple won't hurt. I'll get back on the wagon," he said and headed to the bar.

"He was fine at our last golf game. What the heck happened, Jacquie?" George asked.

Tears filled Jacquie's eyes.

"He was fine. Remember when you called, Martha? Jack had come home at lunch time. He was told he wouldn't be getting the promotion he expected. Instead, they laid him off."

"I guess we have to try and head this off at the pass," George said and strode off after Jack.

The two men who had been roommates in university, were as unalike then as they were now. Jack the athletic, handsome charmer, had turned into a man who looked ten years older and thirty pounds heavier. George, less gregarious than his room-mate, had morphed from a pudgy introvert into a handsome and confident man with the air of what Martha called 'The Elder Statesman.'

Martha realized, for the first time, what George was giving up by retiring.

No wonder he always acts a bit odd when we get together. Jack still treats him like he's the old George, not the man whose words are listened to by some of the most influential people in the country.

Finally in her seat on the airplane, Martha inspected the safety features chart, looked through the complimentary amenity kit, fiddled with seat positions and checked out her video options. George was already asleep. She couldn't hear what Jack and Jacquie were saying, but it seemed that Jack was giving Jacquie grief.

Then, as she reclined her seat and tucked a pillow under her head, she thought she heard Gussy say, "stay the heck out of sight," and wondered why Gussy would be saying that to Frank, but fell asleep before she gave it another thought.

Arrival Day

Marco Polo Airport
Venice, Italy

Martha woke when a gentle hand shook her shoulder.

"Ma'am, we're preparing for our landing in Venice," Martha thanked the flight attendant and quickly gathered her things.

From the terminal, as prearranged by Gussy, they boarded a water taxi, or vaporetto, as she called it. The sleek wooden vessel slipped past the larger Ali Laguna water buses and sped toward their destination.

"Can you believe it, George, we're in Venice," Martha said, nudging her husband.

"What I believe is that I am hungry."

"Seriously?" she said, then dismissed him as Venice came into sight, enthralled by the pastel-hued buildings ornamented with white millwork. They reminded her of frosted cakes. When the pillars of Saint Marc's Square came into view, Martha tried to absorb everything around her.

After checking into the hotel, Gussy told them to 'get a move on,' or they would miss their timed entry to Saint Marc's. She guided them using the GPS on her phone, but Martha noticed that every so often, Gussy would look behind her. At first it seemed like she was making sure they were following her, however, she seemed to fix her gaze on a point behind their group.

Martha turned and scrutinized the people behind them. Her eyes met those of a woman who looked familiar. She caught George's attention, but by the time he turned around all they saw were tourists staring down into their phones no doubt trying to navigate the labyrinthine streets.

"All tourists look the same, Martha. Keep up. If we get lost, the dragon lady will be pissed."

At the Basilica, Martha read inscriptions on the paintings and sculptures and brushed away the group as they tried to hurry her on. Jack demanded they find a place to have a drink. Everyone looked at each other, telegraphing their alarm.

Gussy spoke for them, "I have found us the perfect place for dinner," she said, in a shaky falsetto, and led them to a small restaurant. They were escorted to a table in a flowerpot filled court yard.

· · ·

"GUSSY, YOU'VE REALLY DONE A GREAT JOB OF ORGANIZING THIS TRIP for us," said Frank, raising his glass toward his wife. The rest of the group agreed and raised their glasses saying 'here, here,' and 'great job.'

"Jacquie, you're the only one of us who is still looks fresh as a daisy."

"Oh, thank you, Martha, but if anything, I'm just happy to be here with you guys—and I'm really looking forward to the cruise," Jacquie said as she slowly folded and unfolded the paper band that had been wrapped around her cutlery.

"You bloody well better be," said Jack, "it's costing me a fortune."

Jacquie's head drooped, and Martha stared at Jack in astonishment. Frank had been bringing his wine glass to his mouth. He stopped and put the glass back on the table.

"Jack, your wife works too. Isn't it her money as well as yours that's paying for the trip?"

Jack snorted, "Well you're a fine one to talk. I mean not everyone has a rich wife whose coattails they can ride."

"Riding coat tails, Jack? Is that what it's called when you steal your friend's patents, make a bundle on them and refuse to share?" Frank said.

"Ah, jeez, Frank, let it go. That was years ago," said Jack.

Frank stood up, his chair making a screeching sound on the cobblestones. He was taller, more fit and less inebriated than Jack. Martha hoped they would not come to blows.

"I'll see you guys later; I'm going back to the hotel."

Martha had heard the expression, 'his face grew dark,' but this was the first time she'd seen it.

She knew the two had a dispute back in university during their co-op work term, but had assumed it was over and done with as it had never been brought up during the years of group vacations.

She tried to change the topic, saying she'd almost forgotten they would be embarking on the cruise tomorrow.

No one responded.

On the way back to the hotel, Martha whispered to her husband, "I don't recall him being such a jerk back in school."

"He was okay when he was sober, but when he drank a lot, he could be nasty. Don't you remember the girl he was dating back then? Lizzy? Lisa? And how she said that if he shaved his head, he'd make an awesome prick?" said George.

"Now that you mention it, I do remember."

"It's Jacquie I think we should worry about. He doesn't seem to be treating her well."

Martha was surprised that George had noticed, and reminded herself that her husband could be very kind.

She took his hand, giving it a squeeze. George responded with a smile and returned the squeeze.

EMBARKATION

Cruise Day One, Venice, Italy

"The MSC Sinfonia," Gussy read, as their tender made its way toward the massive ship, "is 177 feet, 2 inches tall, 900 feet long, has 13 decks, with 700 crew and can carry 2,600 passengers."

"Well thank you, Miss Wiki," replied George. Frank snorted. Gussy shot him an annoyed glance.

The friends' cabins were side by side. From their respective balconies they were able to call to each other around white metal partitions. George leaned over and called to Jack and Jacquie, who were in the cabin to his left, and then to Gussy and Frank on the right. He urged his wife to join him watch the Venice coastline as the ship cruised away from the port.

"It's really high up, and looking down at the ocean makes me feel weird," she said.

"I'm with you," said Jack. "I'm not even going out there."

"Yet we will still hear you," said George.

As the ship set sail, the group watched Venice disappear from view.

"Good bye, Venice," Martha said, "I'll be back, I promise."

"We have to report to our muster station in an hour," Gussy called to them, "then we come back to our cabins and get ready for our dinner seating."

Martha tried to focus on the safety speech, but the wind played havoc with her hearing aids. The only thing she took away was that if you fell overboard, you were as good as dead.

Later that evening, George scanned the crowded 'fine dining' restaurant. A waiter approached, looked at their badges, and showed them to a table at the very back of the room. The lights were dim, but Martha could make out Gussy in a sparkly dress. Beside her sat Frank in a plain blue shirt. Jack and Jacquie sat across from them; Jacquie, was in a draped red dress, and Jack wore a lurid palm print shirt.

"Where were you guys?" demanded Gussy as they approached the table, her chandelier earrings brushing the shoulders of her sequinned gown each time she moved her head. Jacquie looked beautiful, yet her makeup did not disguise her red eyes. Her hair was twisted into a type of bun Martha could never master, and her makeup and jewelry, as understated as Martha's, was far more elegant.

Martha tried not to stare, but she was sure she could make out a mark on Jacquie's neck.

Did Jack cause that?

"You look lovely, Jacquie." Martha said hoping the compliment would make her friend smile.

"She bloody well should. You have no idea how long it took her to get ready," Jack said in a loud voice.

"And worth the effort," said George, offering an uncharacteristic compliment. Martha felt grateful that this once, at least, George had been able to read the situation and say the right thing.

"Careful now, George, I might think you have designs on my woman."

"That hair style and the dress suit you, Jacquie," said Martha, "however, you, Jack have clearly not read the dress code."

"Tut, tut," interjected Gussy, "let's enjoy our lovely dinner, then we go to the magic show."

George groaned. "Don't we have an excursion tomorrow? Brindisi was it, Gussy, or did I get my itinerary mixed up?"

"Very funny," Gussy replied, "and don't be a party pooper. The ship docks right at the port so we can wander about as we please. The day after that is a sea day. That's when we recuperate."

At their cabin, George again invited Martha out to the balcony, and this time she joined him, but sat well back from the railing. The moon cast a yellow glowing strip from their ship out to the horizon.

That night she dreamed of walking a yellow path on the ocean.

CRUISE DAY TWO

Brindisi, Italy

"I'm not disembarking," Martha announced at breakfast.

Gussy pouted, "Martha, don't let me down."

"I've got a headache. I'm going to take it easy. Maybe see if I can sleep it off." To everyone's surprise, Frank and Jacquie bowed out as well.

"I've got a few work things to attend to," said Frank, "but the rest of you should go." Jacquie told then that lag has finally caught up with her." George cast a pleading look at Martha, but she refused to be moved.

"Well, then, Gents, it's just the three of us," Gussy said, looking from George to Jack. In the cabin, Martha stretched out on the bed and watched the curtains move with the breeze. She heard voices coming from Frank and Gussy's balcony. It was Frank and Jacquie.

Martha strained to listen, but also felt guilty for eavesdropping. She thought she heard Jacquie say, "it's now or never." Maybe there's something going on between Frank and Jacquie? Then she brushed that thought from her mind. Jacquie and Gussy had been friends long before Martha met them in university.

And Frank was a straight-up guy. There was no way they would hurt Gussy. A few hours later she was feeling better and immersed in an Agatha Christie's They do it with Mirrors when George burst into the cabin, carrying a heavy shopping bag.

"You owe me big time, Martha. That was the day from hell."

"Oh, come on now, it couldn't have been that bad."

"You have no idea. We had to stop at every damn boutique and listen to Gussy telling them what they were doing wrong. She even started rearranging a window display."

George extracted a beer can from the shopping bag and placing the rest in the mini fridge and said, "I'm surprised we weren't escorted back here by police."

· · ·

CRUISE DAY THREE

The Ionian Sea

The ship's decks were full on 'Sea Day,' but the friends were able to find six loungers. Frank and George talked about renovations, Jack slept, snoring slightly, and Gussy and Jacquie had their heads bent close to each other. Martha couldn't hear what they were saying and felt a little left out, then told herself she was being petty, and dove into They do it with Mirrors. Later that evening, she asked George if he'd noticed anything weird in the way Gussy and Frank were treating Jacquie.

"I wouldn't say so. Gussy's always been weird. And Frank, well he's just a nice guy. I think they're both really concerned. Maybe you should talk to Jacquie too. I mean, I would, but you're closer to her. Let her know she's got our support if she needs help."

"Do you think she needs help?"

"I hope not, Martha."

CRUISE DAY FOUR

Mykonos, Greece

The ship sailed through the night and they woke up moored off the Greek island of Mykonos. As soon as they could, the group tendered to shore. Gussy led them to the windmills they'd seen from the port.

After taking several pictures of themselves in front of the windmills, they continued their climb to the highest point in the old city. They hadn't climbed far, but looking down at the blue roofed white houses, Martha could see all of Mykonos below her, and, in the distance, their ship. She walked over to an outcrop, staying well away from the edge, and beckoned the others to join her. They all did, except Jack, who said he was fine where he was.

"In all the years I've known him, I never realized he was afraid of heights," George said to Jacquie.

"Oh yes, it's been a real issue with his work."

"A bridge inspector afraid of heights? How does he do it then?"

Jacquie flashed a fake smile, "Why do you think he drinks?"

That evening, beside the usual printed ship's itinerary left on the bed, was a note. It advised that tomorrow the glass railings would be cleaned and guests should be aware there would be crew out on their balconies.

"No biggie," said Martha, "we're going to be in Athens!"

"Actually, Martha," said George, "according to Gussy's itinerary we will be docking at Piraeus and taking a Hop-on-Hop-off bus to the Acropolis in Athens."

Martha threw a pillow at him. "Just get changed for dinner. I'm hungry."

Cruise Day Five

Piraeus, Greece

The port was busy with buses. The group stood in the shade of a large bus, waiting for their trip from the Port of Piraeus to Athens. The bus trip was longer and hotter than Martha expected.

After they arrived at the Acropolis, they stood in line to wait for tickets, then stood in another line waiting for their number to be called. Finally, they climbed the marble steps up to what

Gussy informed them was the Propylaea, and caught their first sight of the Parthenon. Martha had seen pictures in an encyclopedia, and YouTube videos, but she wasn't prepared for how insignificant it made her feel.

Heat, exertion and hunger were claiming their effects. Martha urged the others to go on while she sought out a shaded spot beside the Temple of Athena. George stayed with her, dabbing her neck with water and fanning her with Gussy's itinerary. "Damn thing is finally useful."

Martha, who had been eating a granola bar, held a finger to her lips. They could hear voices around the corner of the building.

"You have to stop following us," said a woman.

"Everything is set to go. Why are you so worried?"

"You're taking too many chances. You could ruin everything."

"Fine, I'll leave. See you back at the ship, Hon," said the second voice, her steps crunching on stones as she walked away. Martha craned her neck trying to see around the building just as Gussy came around the corner.

"Oh, so this is where you are. Come along, Martha, you at least have to see the view before we leave."

Neither Martha nor George said anything and followed Gussy to a belvedere where they took in a staggering 360-degree view of Athens. Martha was certain one of the women she overheard was Gussy. The opportunity did not arrive for her to confirm this with George.

The return to the ship was a blur. As soon as the bus arrived at the terminal George and Martha headed to the ship while the rest of the friends walked to a nearby cafe. In the cabin she immediately stripped down to her underwear. She was starting to undo her bra when a shadow passed across the balcony.

George quickly interposed himself between her and the glass doors.

"They were supposed to be done with balcony cleaning, weren't they?" Martha hissed.

"I guess not, and why are you whispering? Whoever it was, just walked past. They're gone now."

"I didn't realize the dividers opened up," Martha said, backing into the washroom while keeping George between her and the window.

"You have your shower. I'll go get us some grub," George said.

After her shower, Martha closed the curtains and crawled into bed. She was fast asleep when Geroge got back. She dreamed that she was in a magic show, trying to get in and out of boxes before being sawed into two pieces.

Cruise Day Six

The Adriatic Sea

"Another 'Sea Day,'" George said. He opened the curtains and door to the balcony and stepped outside.

"You really should come out here Martha, the water has changed colour. It's incredibly blue, and you can see lots of little islands and boats…sail boats mainly."

Martha groaned.

"Just let me wake up, then I'll marvel at the view."

"Do you want to join the group or go to the buffet by ourselves?" George asked.

"Neither at the moment. Now that I am somewhat conscious, I want to know what you thought about what we overhead Gussy saying yesterday."

"It might have been Gussy. I mean yeah, she appeared right afterwards, but it could have been anyone. And really, what did we actually hear?"

"I don't know, but it sounded kind of ominous, don't you think?"

"Maybe, but I don't know what to think. The group seems off so nothing surprises me," he replied.

CRUISE DAY SEVEN

Split, Croatia

"Diocletian's Palace, where they filmed scenes for the series Game of Thrones," Gussy read from her guidebook, "was built at the end of the third century AD as a residence for the Roman emperor Diocletian,"

Martha marveled at the stone carvings and watched two actors dressed as Roman soldiers engage in a mock sword fight. Jack pointed out a bar in the square, and the group agreed to a snack and drink. Jack was getting on everyone's nerves.

He was not just nagging Jackie, but irritating his friends with stupid jokes. Before leaving Martha and Jacquie went to the washroom and, while there, Martha asked Jacquie if she was okay.

"Nothing to worry about, Martha. He's an ass, but he's a harmless ass."

"Well, you know, if you need anything…" Martha said.

"Honestly, I'm good. And it's not that much longer," she said.

The trip may not be much longer, but she's got to deal with him back home.

For dinner, they were to dress in white for the ship's theme night. Martha had packed a vintage lace dress she'd thrifted for the occasion, while George wore a blue and white striped polo shirt and jeans saying that he wasn't about to put on a fashion show.

Their friends all in white, were again at the table before George and Martha.

"Am I seeing champagne bottles?" asked Martha.

"Well, yes, Frank and I thought we'd splurge a little," said Gussy, "especially as we have an announcement."

Their friends looked at the couple expectantly.

"Ah, well, how to say this…"

"Augustina Mason? At a loss for words? I don't believe it," said Jack.

"Don't be mean, Jack. Go ahead, Gussy, tell us your news."

"Thank you, Martha," she said, raising her glass to her friend, "so, anyway, as you know, Frank and I have been married for some time. About as long as you guys. And we've raised a wonderful son, who is now raising sons of his own…"

Gussy started tearing up and Frank stepped in.

"It's okay, Gussy, I got this," he said patting his wife's shoulder, "what Gussy is trying to say is that we've had a good thirty years together. And we don't regret that time at all, but…"

"Oh my God," interjected Jack, "you guys are busting up."

"Jesus, Jack. You and your mouth," said George.

"As crass as Jack makes it sound, that is the truth. Gussy and I are separating."

"Sorry, I'm not able to talk about this right now," Gussy said, and left the table. Jacquie immediately stood up and ran after her. Frank apologized, then followed the two women.

"I guess you never really know what goes on behind closed doors," said Martha, glancing from George to Jack. Martha and George ate their meal in silence and left Jack drinking heavily and chatting with the guests at the table next to them.

"I'm not even going to try and stop him," said George. "I'm done."

Martha's head was pounding, so she took one of her strongest migraine pills, flopped on the bed and told George not to get her up for breakfast.

DISEMBARKATION

Cruise Day Eight
Venice, Italy

Martha woke from a nightmare. Her head was pounding. In the moonlight she saw the curtain moving slightly in the breeze.

Damn, we didn't close the sliding glass door.

She reached her arm out, searching for George. In the dim light she could see the sleep apnea machine over his face, sleep mask over his eyes, and she was certain he had put in ear plugs to cover her snoring.

Only an act of God will wake him now.

Hoping to alleviate the pain in her head, she searched for the blister pack of migraine medication on her night stand. She found it, knocking her glasses and hearing aid case onto the floor. Not bothering to search for them, she navigated her way to the refrigerator and reached in for a bottle of water. She sat on the couch, waiting for the pill to take effect, and fell back to asleep.

A sound from the balcony roused her.

She stood up slowly. The cabin was spinning, but her curiosity was roused. She pulled on George's windbreaker, raising the hood over her head then padded over to the sliding glass door and peered through the opening in the curtain. Seeing nothing out of the ordinary, she stepped out onto the balcony cursing herself for not searching for her hearing aids and glasses. The partitions were still open.

Maybe the cleaning crew forgot to close them?

A voice from the left alerted her.

"Jack?" she said, peering into the darkness on Jack and Jacquie's balcony.

"Well, hello, Martha, what bringsh you out on shush a lovely evening?"

"Jack, you're drunk, you should go to bed and sleep it off."

"I'm not afraid of heights, you know. Not at all," he said and climbed onto a chair close to the railing.

"Jesus, Jack, Get down from there."

I'll have you know…" replied Jack's slurred voice, "I am a bridge inshpector, and I can climb way, way higher than this."

Martha watched in horror as he teetered on the chair. She moved quickly, trying to grab him. He wobbled, then flipped over the railing.

She peered down, but saw nothing except glistening darkness below her. She didn't even hear a splash.

Unobserved by Martha, a figure stepped into the shadows and went past George and Martha's balcony, dissolving into the night.

For a moment, Martha was frozen on the spot.

"It's over," she said, then shakily went back to her own balcony, closing the partition behind her. She made her way back to the bed where she was consumed by her own darkness.

"She's waking up," said a male voice speaking English in a strong Italian accent.

Martha pried open her eyes and saw a man in a uniform standing by her bed. Sitting on a chair beside her was a man with a stethoscope. George stood behind him looking down at her. His face still bore the impression of the straps from his sleep apnea machine.

"Martha, thank God. You've been out for hours."

"Sir, please, your wife was in the cabin next to the victim. I need to speak to her without your intervention."

The Doctor spoke. "She's been unconscious from medication. You need to give her time to clear her head."

"What's going on?"

The uniformed man ignored her question.

"Senora, have you been here since you went to bed?"

"Yes," Martha said, nodding her head. "We both were."

"Have you at any time left the cabin?"

"Of course not," said George. "We were both fast asleep until we heard that god-awful siren."

"Senor, please, I'm speaking with your wife."

"I haven't gone anywhere. I took my medication and I was out like a light."

"You didn't hear the alarms?"

"Alarms? No, I don't think so."

"Officer, when she takes a migraine pill, it really does put her out," said George, "One time she slept through a fire alarm when she forgot a pot on the stove and went to bed. Thank God I was home at the time."

"George, what's going on? Why are these men in our cabin?"

George came to her side and bent down. "It's bad, Martha. It seems that Jack has gone overboard."

"Overboard? Have they found him?"

"No, not yet. We've turned around to the spot they think he went over and the Coast Guard are searching."

The Doctor spoke. "Gentlemen, this lady, will be fine, but needs her rest. The medication needs to clear her system before she can answer your questions coherently," the Doctor said, grabbing his bag. "I must check on the victim's wife again. I gave her a sedative and I need to see how she is doing."

The men followed the doctor out of the cabin after the uniformed man issued Martha a warning that he would be back to question her again.

"I don't know what to say, George." Martha leaned back into her pillow, then sat up "What about Jacquie? Where is she?"

"Apparently Jack was nasty so she spent the night on Frank and Gussy's couch."

"Thank God. She's safe," Martha said.

"Just rest. I'll stay here with you," he said laying down beside her. "The thing I don't get, is why was Jack on the balcony? He was afraid of heights."

"False bravado due to alcohol? It is Jack we're talking about."

DETAINMENT

Comando Stazione Carabinieri Marghera
Venice, Italy

The next day they were held by the Carabinieri and asked to recount the events of the evening several times. When they were finally allowed to leave, they were escorted to their hotel while the search continued for Jack.

George and Martha flew home, but Frank and Gussy stayed with Jacquie, sending daily updates, however, Jack's body was never recovered.

A YEAR AND HALF LATER

Home of George and Martha

White Rock, British Columbia

"Hey, George, come and see this," called Martha pointing at the screen of her laptop.

George, carrying the mail, walked into their shared office and asked, "what am I looking at?"

"The woman in the picture with Gussy. Does she look familiar to you?"

George squinted at the screen. "'Having a good time in Santorini with my gal pal, Becky.' Hm. Wasn't the name of her business partner Becky?"

Martha squinted at the screen. "She does look a little like the woman I saw while we were in Italy."

"Really? Are you sure?"

"Not certain."

"Do you think they're a couple? I mean, it could explain the divorce," he replied

"I did not see that coming," Martha said.

"Here's something else you may not have seen coming," said George, handing her a white card.

"'You are cordially invited to the wedding of,'" she gasped, "'Frank and Jacquie?'"

Martha flipped the card over and saw a note. She'd received enough greeting cards from Jacquie to know her hand writing.

We had plans in place, but you gave us the push we needed.

Thank you, Jacquie and Frank

"So, are we going to the wedding or are you going to be too busy reading Sleeping Murder?" George asked pointing at the title of Martha's latest Agatha Christie.

"Actually, George, I think I've had enough Agatha Christie to last a lifetime."

A SAILOR WENT TO SEA

147

ABOUT MERJA TAMMI

Merja's writing explores the tension between the apparent normality of family life and the darker aspects of humanity.

Travel has been a great source for observing people and how they react when out of their 'normal' environment.

She credits her Ottawa writing group, the KFC Scrutineers, with giving her the support and creative encouragement needed to take her writing to the next level.

Merja can be reached at MHTammiWrites@gmail.com.

I.C.U.

Nicola Hamer

I.C.U.

NICOLA HAMER

"Marijke? Marijke? Can you open your eyes?"

Blinking heavy lids, I make out the oval shape of a face, features smeared as though through Vaseline-covered glass. My throat hurts.

"We're taking you to the O.R. to remove the breathing tube. Do you understand? We need to give you general anesthetic, but you'll be more comfortable after that, okay?"

It's possible I nod before closing my eyes.

I HEAR MY MOTHER'S VOICE.

"Marijke? Sweetie? Are you awake?"

Throat still hurts. I cough. Pain splinters through my chest. Gasping, I open my eyes. A round, anxious face hovers.

"Mom?" My voice is a raspy whisper.

"I'm here too, honey." My father's face appears behind my mother's, mirroring her concerned expression. Both of them in the same room, not arguing? Whatever happened to me, it's bad.

I try to sit but my body won't cooperate. More pain: my chest, arms, shooting down my right leg.

"Don't try to sit up." A third voice, with a soft Caribbean lilt.

Looking past my parents, I see a young woman in scrubs, lit by sunlight through the window. A doctor? Nurse? "You've been in a serious accident, and have sustained multiple injuries…"

"But you're going to be okay," my father breaks in. "Don't you worry, honey.

"Let the nurse talk!"

Oh good, there are the parents I recognize.

I focus on the nurse. She asks, "Do you remember the car accident?"

I concentrate. The last thing I remember is calling an Uber for my dentist appointment. I shake my head.

"That's not surprising given your injuries, don't worry. But your father is right, you are going to be just fine, with time."

"What …" I clear my throat, but my voice is still a whisper, "what injuries?"

"Your right thigh is badly broken," the nurse tells me. "You have pins and a frame holding it together until you are strong enough for surgery." I look down at lumps poking up under the blanket over my right leg.

"Your abdomen was perforated, but only your colon was affected. You sustained a small tear of approximately four centimeters. The doctor performed a colostomy to allow it to heal, but it's likely only temporary, and you will be able to have it reversed later."

"Colostomy?"

The nurse gently pushes up my blue hospital gown. My previously perfect, flat belly is split by a jagged, stapled incision running from my belly button down to my pubic bone. A small plastic bag rests on the lower left side of my stomach. She fiddles with it, then lifts the bag to reveal a circle of soft, pink tissue. It's surrounded by a bandage with pieces of plastic attached.

"This is a stoma," the nurse explains, "where the doctor sewed the healthy end of your colon. Feces now exit into this bag." She points to the bandage around a circle of pink intestine. "This is called a flange, and it holds the bag in place." Placing the bag over the flange, she manipulates it until I feel a soft click.

Okay, I can't walk, and I shit in a bag.

"Anything else?"

"The perforation led to an infection that you are still fighting. That's why you have this drainage tube." She indicates a tube protruding from my lower abdomen. I try to crane my neck to follow the tube over the edge of the bed and pain shoots through my head and right shoulder. "You also have pneumonia and a number of significant contusions, particularly around your right shoulder."

"How long have I been here?"

"A week. You've been in a medically induced coma during that time." The nurse pulls my gown back down. "I know this is a lot to take in, but do you have any questions for me?"

My mind is fuzzy.

She places a warm, reassuring hand on my arm. "You've been through a lot. Just rest."

I close my eyes.

The room is dim, lit only by a small bedside lamp. A familiar figure is curled in the chair beside my bed, face lit by her phone.

"Ellie?" I rasp, throat so dry it hurts.

Ellie is beside me in a flash, gently pushing my hair from my face.

"Marijke! Oh, babe, I was so worried. I'm so glad you are awake!" Her large brown eyes fill with tears.

The dryness catches at my throat, and I cough. Again, my chest explodes.

"Water?"

Grabbing the water glass from my bedside tray, Ellie holds the straw to my mouth. I suck eagerly and choke. Each cough is a boot-kick. *Note to self: never cough again.*

"Easy. Tiny sips, okay?"

Once I can breathe, I obey. The soreness eases.

"Better." My voice isn't as raspy, but still not much above a whisper. "Can you tell me about the accident?"

Ellie's normally sunny face grows dark. "Some fucker T-boned you! Right though the light and smashed into the car at, like, 60 kilometres an hour."

I blink, trying to picture it.

"Your driver was basically fine. I think the other guy had some injuries, but nothing like you. I got this call from the hospital…" Ellie shudders. "That was awful. And then I had to call your parents…"

The door opens and a portly, middle-aged nurse bustles in holding two IV bags and an iPad.

"Hello, ladies! I'm Mrs. Bouchard, and I will be your nurse all night," she says cheerfully, setting the bags and iPad down on my rolling tray. Then she looks at me. "I'm guessing you are Marijke," she teases.

"You pronounced her name right!" Ellie cheers.

"I had another patient with that name," Mrs. Bouchard explains, a sad look passing fleetingly across her face. I change the subject.

"Are those bags both for me?" I turn my head, trying to see what she has started to do beyond my left shoulder.

"They are!"

"You have all kinds of stuff back there," Ellie tells me. "It's impressive." She takes a photo, and then turns her phone to show me. I'm shocked at the bank of machines behind the bed.

"Oh," I say, overwhelmed.

"Don't you worry, dear," says Mrs. Bouchard. "We're taking good care of you! See, I even have dinner." She grins and produces a small bottle of Ensure from her pocket. I grimace. The nurse cracks the cap and hands it to me. "Can you hold it steady?"

My hands are not part of me. They ignore my brain and shake uncontrollably. Tears fill my eyes.

"Oh now, none of that," the nurse says gently, taking the bottle and opening it. "It's to be expected. It'll come back quickly, I promise."

Still, my tears overflow.

"I don't know why I'm crying."

Ellie hugs me and wipes my face. Mrs. Bouchard holds the Ensure to my lips. "Can you take a sip for me?" I sip, and grimace again.

"Disgusting."

"Hopefully tomorrow the doctor will sign off on solid food," the nurse tells me as she pours more of the drink into my mouth.

She turns to Ellie. "Can I ask you to step out for a moment while I change Marijke's colostomy bag? You can come back in a few minutes." Ellie gently squeezes my hand and stands up.

"You just let me do the work," the nurse says.

I lay my head back and close my eyes.

THE ROOM IS DARK. I BLINK UP AT THE CEILING, TRYING TO ORIENT myself. Hospital, I am in the hospital. My leg hurts. My shoulder hurts. My belly hurts. My throat hurts. I try to swallow but cannot muster the saliva.

There's a full glass of water on the table beside my bed. Even as I lift my shaking arm, I realize that attempting to pick it up will result in water spilling everywhere, but I'm desperate enough to try. My fingers touch the damp glass but refuse to curl around it, much less pull it towards me. My arm drops back to my side, and I feel the prick of tears.

It occurs to me to call the nurse, but when I spot the call button, it's clipped to the bedframe at my right. I glare at it, so tantalizingly close. For all I can reach it, it might as well be a thousand miles away, along with the water.

I consider calling out, but I still haven't the strength to speak much above a whisper.

Sighing, I close my eyes, trying to ignore my throat and get back to sleep.

SUDDENLY, A TALL YOUNG MAN IN SCRUBS WALKS TOWARDS ME. I don't think I slept, but I didn't notice him come in. His wavy, dark hair partly obscures his face, and I cannot catch his eyes. Without a glance, he moves past me to the machines behind my head.

"Can I please have some water?" I whisper. He ignores me. "Just, when you are done with that?"

Still no response, and I don't want to be a nuisance. I close my eyes and take several slow breaths to keep calm, willing myself to be patient. When I open them, he's gone. Tears of frustration fill my eyes once again.

Something behind my head begins to beep. Moments later, the door to my room opens to admit Mrs. Bouchard.

"Time for a new bag!" she announces, as cheerful as earlier.

"May I have some water?" I cannot restrain my eagerness.

"Of course!" She holds the straw to my mouth. I drink gratefully, remembering to only take small sips.

"Thank you. I don't want to be a nuisance, but my mouth

gets so dry. I asked the other nurse – doctor? – but I guess he didn't hear me."

"I'm the only nurse here, dear, but don't you worry about being a nuisance." She gestures to the call button. "You and your neighbour are my only patients, so you call me any time."

"I can't reach it."

"Whoops! Let's fix that." She moves the call button and makes sure I'm comfortable before leaving. I fall into a peaceful sleep.

THE NEXT MORNING, I LAY STARING OUT THE WINDOW. I'M TRYING to focus on questions for the doctor when I hear Ellie's voice outside my room. Then I recognize the childish voice of Willow, her 6-year-old niece. Odd that children are allowed in the ICU. I watch the door, anticipating their appearance. It doesn't open. Maybe it isn't yet visiting hours?

I wait. Voices fade in and out, but I can't understand the words. Finally, the door opens, but only a nurse enters, introducing herself as Keiko.

"Good morning ..." she peers intently at my chart. "Mari..gee...key?" I will literally never forgive my parents for giving me a 'unique' name.

"It's pronounced Mar-aye-ka. It's Dutch," I say, for the seven billionth time in my life.

"Pretty name." She begins to check my incision and colostomy. "You're getting a sponge bath this morning. Aren't you lucky!"

"Can it maybe wait?" I ask her. "I heard my girlfriend outside."

"It's not quite visiting hours." She sounds regretful. "But I didn't see anyone out there." She's changed the IV bags and is now headed into the bathroom to fill a basin of water.

"But I heard her …" I say as she returns. I'm confused.

"Well, I'm sure she'll be back soon. Now let's get that gown off."

Instead of Ellie, visiting hours produce my parents, eager to be here when the doctor arrives. I don't like their babying. But after Dr. Gaury, a stern-looking middle-aged man, appears, I change my mind. They clearly find it easy to follow his words, only by the time I've absorbed one fact, they've already moved on. I feel trapped inside my head by my malfunctioning body.

"Your recovery is progressing well," Dr. Gaury says. "We should be able to remove the drainage tube soon, and then we can get on with fixing your leg. Feel like eating something?"

I do not, in fact, feel like eating anything. But if it helps me avoid Ensure I'll give it a go, and say as much. Promising to have the nurse bring in breakfast, the doctor leaves.

The plain Cheerios and bran muffin are only marginally more appetizing than the Ensure.

I close my eyes as my mother is talking about … Thailand?

I am staring vacantly out the window, not blinking. I'm aware this is a new ability: to sit inside my head, barely interacting with the world, no other thoughts. It's strange; I should be doing something, maybe reading one of the magazines on my tray. And yet, I just sit.

I have no idea how much time passes before I manage to blink, focus my eyes, and look around the room.

A woman is sitting silently beside my bed. I startle, then focus on her. She looks to be in hard-won middle age. Her drawn, pale face appears dry, almost papery. Her faded red hair hangs just past her shoulders, and an old-fashioned nurse's cap sits on her head.

Seeing me look at her, the nurse smiles, revealing yellowed teeth. She reaches out one bird-like hand, thin skin pulled tight over bones, and strokes my hair. I don't like it and try to pull away.

"You can see me," she says, almost to herself. Her dry rasp rivals mine.

"Yeah. It's not like I'm still in the coma." I know I am being snippy, but she gave me a shock and it's a stupid thing to say. Obviously, I can see her.

"It's okay. Rest more."

"Can you help me get comfortable? Maybe raise the bed a bit?"

"Close your eyes. Rest," she repeats.

I don't feel particularly tired, but I do feel helpless. I close my eyes obediently and, as it seems to do here, sleep comes quickly.

I WAKE INTO DARKNESS, SORE AND THIRSTY. STARING AT THE ceiling, I try to remember what to do. I know the answer is simple, if only I can focus.

Before I work it out, in walks the man from the night before. He's about my age and good looking: tan skin, even features, and that thick black hair. But he has dark circles of exhaustion around his eyes and a face creased with worry.

This time, I catch his name tag before he reaches the machines behind my head and gets to work doing ... whatever he needs to do: Dr. Pender.

"Can I have some water?" Like last night, he ignores me.

Needles of irritation prick at me. He might not be a nurse, but does he have to ignore me completely?

"Can you at least send in the nurse?" At this, he turns and walks away. Jerk.

I close my eyes and try to relax. I'm fading, almost asleep, when I begin to hear music.

Dancing queen, young and sweet, only 17…

I recognize the ABBA song and start to bop my head slightly to the tune, spirits somewhat lifted. Then another song, and this time I hear the nurses singing along. From nowhere, I realize the nurses are decorating each ICU room in a different theme, representing different countries. *What a good idea to help cheer people up.* As I drift back to sleep, I wonder what theme my room will be. Hawaiian would be nice …

I'M DISAPPOINTED THAT THE NURSES DIDN'T REACH MY ROOM LAST night. Still plain hospital bland. Ellie arrives and I tell her about the decorations. She stares at me, concern on her face.

"Wait, are you telling me that the nurses spent their time last night partying and decorating rooms?"

"I'm sure just in their spare time," I say, sipping the homemade soup Ellie reheated for me. The tumbler has a lid and straw, allowing me to hold it myself. Nurse Bouchard was right: already I'm shaking less.

"If they didn't reach you, how do you know what they were doing? You can't see into any other room."

That gives me pause and I consider.

"I'll grant you it's a bit weird," I say. "But I remember it."

"I'll be right back." Ellie hops from her chair and leaves the room, then returns moments later. "I looked. The other rooms look the same as yours."

I glare at her. "But. I. Remember. It."

The nurse arrives. I remember her from the first day. Her name tag says Rose.

"Oh good!" says Ellie. "Maybe you can help us with something. Marijke remembers the nurses last night playing music and decorating the rooms, but I looked and none of the room are decorated."

When she puts it like that, it does seem unlikely. But I *remember* it.

Rose comes over to check my bandages, asking, "Did you actually see any of this?"

I think about it. I remember the different rooms, but I realize it's impossible for me to have seen what I remembered. I must look as confused as I feel because she gives me a kind smile.

"Don't worry about it. You are probably experiencing ICU psychosis."

Ellie looks shocked. "Psychosis!"

"It's quite common, and nothing to be concerned about," Rose explains. "Most ICU patients have undergone significant physical trauma and are on multiple medications. This can cause hallucinations, both visual and auditory. It fades by the time they leave us."

"That explains some things," I say, thinking of Ellie and Willow talking outside my door, but never showing up.

*Okay, I shit in a bag, can't walk, **and** I am imagining things. Great.*

Next time I wake up, the nurse with the old-fashioned cap is sitting in the chair in the corner of my room. Seeing that I'm awake, she approaches. Like before, she reaches her bony hand towards my hair.

"We'll take good care of you." She sounds like a five-pack-a-day smoker. I have always found it strange when medical professionals smoke. She smiles, and I notice her lipstick has mostly rubbed from her lips, leaving them pale, but with bright red in the cracks and wrinkles of her mouth. The result is a smile more disturbing than reassuring.

"Okay," I say, uncertain. Then I remember what Rose said about the hallucinations. Despite the strangeness of the question, I ask, "Are you real?"

Her laugh is a dry crackle. "What a strange question. After all, you can see me."

She stops stroking my hair and her hand lightly drifts down my arm. It creates an unpleasant ticklish feeling, like a spider crawling. She returns to the chair. "Sleep. I'll keep you company." *Since when do nurses keep you company?* Hallucination.

I don't want to close my eyes, but my eyelids are so heavy.

THE NIGHT PASSES WITH NO MORE MUSIC OR DECORATING NURSES. It's too bad. I liked the music, even if it was only in my head. Rude Dr. Pender is on duty again, but I don't even bother trying to talk to him.

The next morning, Mrs. Bouchard removes the drainage tube and tells me I'm strong enough for the surgery on my leg. Instead of the metal on the outside of my leg, I will have a rod inside.

"I guess that's good," I say, not looking forward to surgery.

"It definitely is," she assures me, and says she'll return soon to prepare me.

BY THE EVENING, I'M BACK IN MY ROOM, WITHOUT THE METAL sticking out of my leg. As I'm trying to count the number of staples closing the incision running from hip to knee, Ellie arrives, walking around the bed and coming face-to-surgical-wound.

"Whoa! That's a lot of staples!"

I laugh weakly. "Tomorrow, I get my catheter out. Then I get to try standing."

"They don't waste time here." She hands me my nightly tumbler of homemade soup.

"No," I say, taking a sip. Cream of mushroom. "And yet it still feels like I have been here forever."

WHEN MY MOTHER IS LATE FOR HER MORNING VISIT, THE NURSE pronounces me ready to feed myself. She drapes a towel over me, then balances the bowl of Cheerios and milk on my chest and hands me a spoon.

"Be back soon!" she says - far too cheerfully - and leaves.

I hold the spoon in a closed-fisted toddler grip and manage to scoop up some cereal. My hand shakes. I manoeuvre the spoon towards my face, dribbling a trail of liquid between bowl and mouth. With the next scoop, I knock the spoon against the bowl and milk sloshes onto my chest.

"This is so fun," I announce to the empty room.

As I soldier on, I begin to notice barking from the hallway, and children laughing. "Thank you so much," I hear a man say. "What a great place to have a dog adoption centre." There's a deep 'woof' that sounds like a Great Dane. I decide to ask the nurse when she returns if a dog can visit me.

It takes a long time to empty the bowl. At least half the milk and cereal are on my chest, and I'm chilled through by the time the nurse returns to change both me and the bedsheets. *Probably would have taken less time to just feed me,* I think, somewhat vengefully, as I shiver.

As she moves to efficiently and painlessly remove my catheter, it comes to me that I no longer hear barking. I suddenly realize that the idea of adopting dogs from the ICU is utterly absurd. I almost smack myself in the forehead, it's so ridiculous.

But moments before, it seemed completely reasonable. Apparently, in the midst of a hallucination, I won't necessarily be aware of it.

It's discomforting to realize that, in the moment, I won't know what's real.

I'M STARING OUT AT THE RAIN, WAITING FOR THE NURSE FROM rehabilitation therapy to arrive. I lose track of time, again. When I come back to the world, I turn to look at the clock and spot the creepy nurse sitting quietly in the chair in the corner. Flinching in surprise again, I become irritated. This is one hallucination I am certainly aware of in the moment.

"You're just a figment of my imagination." I glare at her. "You should fuck off."

She responds with that yellow-toothed grin.

"Don't worry. I will look after you."

I roll my eyes and decide to ignore her, grabbing my phone to text Ellie. Thank the phone gods for voice recognition software.

Moments later, several nurses arrive, bringing a walker and weird-looking chair with them. I spare a quick glance at the chair in the corner. Empty. *Good. Stay gone.*

The rehab nurses explain that standing does not equal walking. Right now, my goal is to hold onto the walker and shift my body 90 degrees. That way I can sit down on the weird chair, which turns out to be a portable commode. I sigh as I stand back up and wait for a nurse to wipe me. I wonder when progress will stop being accompanied by fresh humiliation?

AGAIN, I WAKE IN THE MIDDLE OF THE NIGHT AS DR. PENDER enters my room. Instead of ignoring him, I switch tactics and greet him with as much enthusiasm as I can muster.

"Hello Dr. Pender! How are you tonight?"

To my surprise, without fully turning his head in my direction, he shifts his gaze from the machines to focus his dark, deep-set, eyes on mine. In the dim light, his eyes appear large and featureless. He stares at me silently for several unblinking moments before turning his attention back to the equipment.

I decide being ignored is preferable to that gaze and close my eyes.

I don't hear him leave, but a few minutes later, Keiko enters, carrying an IV bag.

"What's up with Dr. Pender?" I ask. "He's so rude."

She glances up sharply, looking surprised. "Who?"

"Dr. Pender. He was just here."

She stares at me for several beats, blinking rapidly. "There's... there's no doctor with that name working here."

I blink right back at her, trying to process what she said.

"But I saw him. I've seen him every night." Damn, another hallucination?

"Has anyone discussed ICU psychosis with you?"

Yup, another hallucination. Except ...

"Yes, I know about it. But when I asked you about Dr. Pender, it seemed like you knew the name."

Keiko busies herself checking my vitals.

"Keiko?

She glances up at me, then back down at her iPad for a moment before apparently deciding to be straight with me.

"There was someone who used to work here with that name, but he hasn't been here for several years."

"Maybe he's returned?"

She looks away. Are those tears I see glinting in her eyes?

"No. He's dead."

* * *

I dream I'm in my kitchen, facing a pile of dirty dishes. As I grab one to load the dishwasher, a black spider appears and skitters up my arm. Startled, I shake and the spider drops. But even as it hits the floor, another appears, and then another, scuttling along my arm.

Suddenly, I'm awake, blinking into the morning light. I close my eyes against the brightness and realize the crawling sensation on my arm isn't fading. I open them to see bony fingers trailing lightly along my forearm and gaze up at a now-familiar tired face, sunlight glinting off faded hair and that ridiculous nurse's cap. Where have I seen one of those before to add this to my hallucination?

I wave irritably. "I thought I told you to fuck off."

She gives me a smile that might have otherwise seemed kind, were it not for the slivers of red lipstick like shards between the wrinkles of her lips.

"It's my job to care for you," she rasps.

"Yeah, yeah," I manoeuvre a pillow between my legs to lie on my side, turning my back on her. I feel a slight tugging on my hair. I'm momentarily confused, then realize it must be her hand, smoothing my hair back.

The feeling makes me shiver and I concentrate on ignoring it. I'm finally fading to sleep when a thought pops into my head: the nurse talked about *seeing* imaginary things and *hearing* imaginary things. She never mentioned *feeling* imaginary things. Suddenly fully awake, I glance behind me, heart thudding.

There's no one there.

"I'm still having hallucinations," I tell Mrs. Bouchard. She's leaning close, focusing on my upper chest as she carefully removes an IV tube.

"Getting rid of the central line IV means you're improving," she says. "But I need to replace it with a regular one in your hand, unfortunately. You aren't quite free of the meds yet."

"Okay." I pause. "But is the hallucination thing weird? Shouldn't they be gone by now?" Obligingly, I hold up my arm for her to wrap with elastic tubing and watch her tap along the vein on my hand.

"Not necessarily, dear. You'll be in the ICU for at least another day or two." She gestures with her chin to where the central line had entered my chest only moments before. "Also, you literally *just* got off the heavy-duty meds."

She swipes the back of my hand with an alcohol wipe.

"Deep breath in."

Obediently, I suck in air, letting it out as I feel the needle pierce my skin.

"Okay, but is it normal to hallucinate the same thing? Like, the same person, but at different times?"

The nurse tapes the IV to my hand and turns her gaze on me. Still holding my hand, she says, "The truth is there is no 'normal' when it comes to what someone hallucinates. You wouldn't believe the stories we've heard!" She laughs.

Focusing on my hand in hers, I ask, "What about hallucinating feeling something, like a touch?"

"It's not as common, but I've heard that too."

Her warm hands and kind voice are reassuring. I sigh deeply, tension releasing with my expelled breath, and give her a small smile.

"Okay. Thank you. I feel better, although I wish they would just go away. Also, I really wish I hadn't incorporated a real doctor's name into a hallucination."

"Oh?" Mrs. Bouchard scoops up the packaging and old IV tubing. "Which doctor?"

"No one I know." I tell her, exasperated. "Some old guy who is already dead. Dr. Pender."

"Oh, that was awful. Everyone was so upset when he died." She tosses the garbage, then goes into the bathroom to dampen a cloth before returning to remove my full colostomy bag. "But he certainly wasn't 'some old guy.'" She smiles wistfully as she washes my stoma. "He was a young man, so handsome. It was such a tragedy the way he killed himself. And here in the hospital too!"

"He … he killed himself?"

She shakes her head sadly. "It can take a lot out of you, working in the ICU. We lose patients more often than we'd like. No wonder it's taking some staff members a good long time to get over it, and I wouldn't be surprised if you overheard them talking about it, especially given your name."

"My name?"

"We had a patient with the same name. Her death wasn't his fault, but still…"

She trails off, then gives herself a little shake, clicks my new bag into place, and pats me on the leg.

"But you are going to be just fine, dear."

And with that, she leaves me alone.

THANKFULLY, I AVOID ANOTHER VISIT FROM DR. PENDER BY sleeping through the night for the first time since I woke up in the ICU. When the creepy nurse doesn't appear and nothing bizarre happens all the next day, I begin to hope I'm done with the hallucinations. Best of all, at the end of the day the nurse tells me my pneumonia has cleared and I can move to the rehab floor in the morning. I smile, feeling a sense of progress.

MY MOTHER ARRIVES WITH A BOX AND EFFICIENTLY PACKS UP THE photos, phone charger, and knickknacks I have accumulated. I bid a heartfelt farewell to Keiko, asking her to pass along my thanks to the other nurses. Off we go, orderly pushing my wheelchair, to the rehabilitation wing.

As soon as I'm settled, a new nurse appears. She has a firm expression and tightly curled salt-and-pepper hair. With a no-nonsense tone, she introduces herself as Linda.

"What do we have here?" she asks, looking me over and picking up my chart.

"Broken thigh," I say ruefully, as though it's somehow my fault.

"Right," she puts down my chart. "Feel like going for a pee?"

My new room has a handicap-accessible bathroom. I look at it, so far away. I haven't yet taken more than a couple of steps in a row.

My mother tries to take charge. "She hasn't walked before. Don't you think that's pushing it?" This has the opposite effect than intended, at least on me.

"Okay," I tell the nurse, as I snag my walker and drag it to where I'm sitting on the bed.

"Do you need my help standing up?" My mother hovers over me.

"No, Mom. We already discussed this, remember? The other nurses taught me how to do it myself."

I rock back and forth to gain momentum, then push myself to standing. I look at my one young, normal foot and my one old-lady foot, swollen and purple, and sigh. Then I focus on the bathroom and take one determined step, then another.

"Take your time," Linda says, standing at my elbow.

"I don't know if …"

"Mom! Enough!"

Three steps, four. The initial pain in my right foot starts to ease. Six steps and I reach the bathroom door. Two more and I've made it to the toilet. I grin proudly at the nurse.

"Good job," she says seriously, watching me shuffle until I'm facing the right direction.

"I've got it from here," I say, having graduated to pulling up my own underwear yesterday.

The walk back to bed is slower, but no less determined. I collapse onto it and announce I need a nap. The nurse leaves, but my mother fusses.

"Are you sure you will be okay by yourself? You won't get the same level of attention as you did in the ICU."

"I'm fine," I say dismissively. "This is progress!"

Then a raspy voice says, "Don't worry. I'll take good care of her."

I look towards the sound. There she is, sitting in the chair in the corner, adjusting her cap.

I sigh, deeply disappointed I'm not yet free of the hallucinations after all. Also, they've never before shown up when I'm with someone…

"Mom, I have a kind of crazy question for you."

My mother looks up from digging in her purse for her keys.

"Do you see anyone in that chair?" I point towards the corner.

My mother glances over, then back at me. "Is this a trick question?"

"Mom, just answer, okay?"

She gives a little laugh. "Of course not. I'll see you later. Don't try walking alone!" And with that, she's gone, and it's just me and Creepy Nurse.

I WAKE UP IN THE NIGHT, BUT TO MY RELIEF, DR. PENDER DOESN'T return. *Maybe he sticks to the ICU?* I shake my head. *Hallucination, remember?*

. . .

ELLIE AND I ARE CUDDLING IN MY BED, ONE EYE ON THE DOOR FOR the nurse, who does not approve of my girlfriend in my bed. Also, my parents are supposed to arrive soon to be here for my occupational therapy appointment.

A young man in scrubs stops momentarily in front of my door, glancing in, but then moves on. I'm trying to figure out why he looks so familiar when I am distracted by the arrival of a young woman who should be on a fashion runway but introduces herself as the occupational therapist. She's familiarizing herself with my chart when my parents appear.

She asks me a lot of questions about our apartment. How many steps are involved in getting inside? How big is the bathroom? How much help will I have?

Ellie looks distraught, saying, "I work full-time. Shift work." At the same time, I realize how small our place is; manoeuvring with a walker will be difficult.

We share a mournful look.

"We have a ground floor guest room!" My mother could not look more delighted. "You can stay as long as you need! And since I'm retired, I'll be around to help you." She beams.

"Now Beth, don't coddle her." My father's voice is stern.

"I'm not coddling!" snaps my mother. "The doctor here just said she needs help." She scowls at him.

"I'm an occupational therapist," says the occupational therapist. She then gives me a sympathetic smile. "It does sound like staying at your parents' place for a while is the right move."

Ellie squeezes my hand. "Only for a little while, babe."

"Only for a little while," I agree with a sigh.

. . .

WHEN I WAKE UP IN THE NIGHT, DR. PENDER IS BESIDE ME, apparently fiddling with my IV. His dark eyes flick towards me.

"Sorry," he mumbles, barely audible, as I stare at him in shock. "It took me some time to find you." It's then that I realize why the guy in scrubs looked so familiar.

I watch him walk from the room.

"I think I'm losing my mind," I tell the empty room, and burst into tears.

"I'M STILL KIND OF HAVING HALLUCINATIONS," I SAY TO MY NURSE the next morning. A big, bearded man with a surprisingly gentle manner, he's setting up supplies to teach me how to change the bandage thingie around my colostomy stoma. He glances up with a confused expression.

"You know, like ICU psychosis?"

"I get that. But 'kind of?'"

"These ones seem ... different. Most of them were silly, like hearing dogs being adopted or music, and they didn't last long. But the ones sticking around are just ... people. And they keep coming back."

"Like, you keep seeing the same people?"

"Yes. Is that weird?"

"I don't think it's common, but it must happen." He opens the package with the new bandage thingie and places it in front of me.

Tears begin to well. "It feels like ..." I feel silly saying the words. "It feels like I'm being haunted."

"That must be hard," he says sympathetically. "But remember that you've been through a traumatic event. Healing takes time."

"What if my brain is just broken?" I swipe at my eyes.

"It's not broken, just a little beaten up. You'll be okay." He points to my stoma. "Now, can you peel your old flange off? Just hold the skin and pull up gently."

I blink back the tears and focus on my belly, holding my skin down as ordered and pulling the flange free. *Just a little beaten up, I tell myself as I press the new flange into place. You'll be okay.*

"YOU AREN'T BEING HAUNTED AND YOU AREN'T CRAZY," ELLIE SAYS, giving my good shoulder a gentle shove. "Well, no crazier than you were before."

"Tell that to Creepy Nurse." I gesture towards the chair, where she sits placidly, playing with her stringy hair.

"You see her right now?"

"Uh-huh. Lately, she's always around." Ellie stares intently at the chair for a moment. "She also talks to me. 'I'll always take care of you'." I mimic her raspy voice.

"That *is* creepy. Also, bullshit. I am the one who gets to take care of you." Seeing my miserable expression, she pulls me into a hug. I close my eyes and melt into her arms, then open them again as she grabs her hat from the bedside table and says with playful bravado, "Take that, Creepy Nurse," and flings it at the chair. The empty chair.

I snuggle more deeply into the safety of Ellie's arms, and smile.

FINALLY, I AM DEEMED STRONG ENOUGH TO LEAVE THE HOSPITAL. Even though I'm going to my childhood home rather than the adult apartment I share with my adult girlfriend, I'm eager to be sprung and in a great mood. Fresh air! Real food! No one loudly asking me about my bowel movements!

My parents keep the bickering to a minimum as we pack my few belongings. As my father pushes my wheelchair down the hall, my belongings in my lap and my mother trailing behind, we encounter Mrs. Bouchard. She greets me with a wide smile.

"Look at you, on your way home! You definitely look healthier than the last time I saw you."

I smile up at her. "Definitely feel better too. The I.C.U. is already feeling like a distant memory."

"And how about those pesky hallucinations?"

My smile widens. I haven't seen anything strange in days. "Those too."

"See?" Mrs. Bouchard tells me. "Before you know it, this whole experience will be a distant memory."

And then my father is pushing me down the hall again, and out into the sunshine.

When we reach the curb, I lock the brakes of my wheelchair and wait with my mother while my father heads into the parking lot for the car.

Standing to my right, my mother prattles on about lunch with Aunt Louise. I become aware of movement on my left. I look up at the man in scrubs and his eyes flick towards me for the briefest moment. My body goes cold.

Unable to speak, I watch Dr. Pender glance over his left shoulder as Creepy Nurse joins us, a cigarette between her lips. She takes a long puff, then holds it towards Dr. Pender, who accepts it. Then she cranes her neck past him and favours me with a wide smile, sunlight glinting off flecks of red.

"You still see me … and I will always take care of you."

As I struggle to absorb what I am seeing, Dr. Pender appears to take a deep drag, the end of the cigarette flaring. Smoke drifts between him and Creepy. Without exhaling, he takes another, then turns towards me.

His hair is pushed behind his ear, and there's a hole in the side of his face. Transfixed, I watch the smoke curl past the ragged, bloody flesh and dissipate in the breeze.

I turn away from the sight as father's car pulls up. As I wiggle into the back seat, I tell myself firmly: *I'm leaving all this behind.*

I look out the window at the empty sidewalk and sigh with relief, then lower it so I can take in fresh air as I watch the medical buildings retreat.

I suck in a deep lungful of air, but instead of the fresh smell I expect, the faint odour of cigarette smoke reaches my nostrils. I feel as though my heart has stopped. I keep my eyes closed and try to slow my breathing. All I can think is *no, no, no.* Then I open my eyes.

They are beside me in the car. Dr. Pender's dark eyes catch mine.

"I'm not going to lose you this time."

-\ -

ABOUT NICOLA HAMER

With a master's in History and one in Journalism, Nicola Hamer has been writing her entire life. However, only recently has she turned back to an old love, writing fiction.

She is now hard at work on her first novel.

I.C.U. is her first published short story and is based - almost entirely - on her own experiences many years ago.

When not writing, Nicola gardens, carves soapstone, knits, cross-stitches, spends time with her husband and partners and many pets and enjoys watching her four mostly adult children mostly adult very successfully.

PLEASE LEAVE A REVIEW!

If you enjoyed this collection of short stories, could you please leave us a quick review? We would appreciate it!

You can leave a review on any or all of these sites:

Amazon

Goodreads

BookBub

Thank you!

ABOUT THE KFC SCRUTINEERS

The KFC Scrutineers is an Ottawa-based writing group whose members share creative goals and like-minded focus on reaching their personal artistic ideals. Through critique, encouragement, and laughter, each contributor improves the other, uniting us in the written word.

The authors in the group hail from Canada, the USA, and Finland.

Other books by KFC Scrutineers:

Seven Deadly Pens 1

A Write Christmas

www.ingramcontent.com/pod-product-compliance
Lightning Source LLC
Chambersburg PA
CBHW032026050726
47590CB00006B/2314